Night Flower

The Coventry Adams Mysteries, Volume 1

Steven Henry

Published by Clickworks Press, 2026.

Table of Contents

For Professor James McDonnell, who taught the
smallest and most interesting 19th-Century Literature
class I ever took.

"Forlorn men, women, and children—and a spacious township peopled with them, from cellars to attics—from the resort of the sewer rat to the nest of the sparrow in the chimney-stack—make up that realm of suffering and crime..."

— Gustav Dorè and Blanchard Jerrold

London: A Pilgrimage (1872)

Copyright © 2026 Steven Henry

Cover design © 2026 Wahyu Ganiswara

Author photo © 2017 Shelley Paulson Photography

All rights reserved

First publication: Clickworks Press, 2026

Release: CWP-COV01-INT-P.IS-1.0

Sign up for updates, deals, and exclusive sneak peeks at clickworkspress.com/join.

Ebook ISBN: 979-8-88900-041-9

Paperback ISBN: 979-8-88900-042-6

Hardcover ISBN: 979-8-88900-043-3

This is a work of fiction. Names, characters, places, organizations, and events are either the products of the author's imagination or used in a fictitious manner. Any resemblance to actual persons, living or dead, is purely coincidental.

Also by Steven Henry

The Coventry Adams Mysteries
Night Flower
Thief-Taker (coming soon)

The Erin O'Reilly Mysteries
Black Velvet
Irish Car Bomb
White Russian
Double Scotch
Manhattan
Black Magic
Death By Chocolate
Massacre
Flashback
First Love
High Stakes
Aquarium
The Devil You Know
Hair of the Dog
Punch Drunk

Bossa Nova
Blackout
Angel Face
Tequila Sunrise: A James Corcoran Story
Italian Stallion
White Lightning
Kamikaze
Jackhammer
Frostbite
Brain Damage
Celtic Twilight
Headshot
Vino Blanco
White Lady
Blackjack
Last Round

Standalone
Fathers: A Modern Christmas Story

**For reminders and updates from Steven Henry,
sign up at clickworkspress.com/join/steven.**

Chapter 1

The gaslights glowed in the fog like will-o-the-wisps, ghostly and eerie. The fog was a thick, tangible thing. Even in the most crowded streets, it gave the illusion of solitude. And London's streets were very crowded. One was rarely alone, even now, near midnight. The muffled clop of horse-hooves echoed constantly on the cobbles and the hushed murmur of voices came from the doors and windows of a hundred public-houses.

Coventry sniffed the air. She smelled coal smoke, unwashed bodies, cheap scent, litter, and horse dung. She wondered how many horses lived and worked in London. Too many, toiling in the filthy, stony streets. Would any of them wish to remain, given the choice, when open pastures beckoned?

A rib of whalebone pinched her just below the ribs. She winced and shifted in her corset, trying to find a more comfortable position. She was fortunate she was such a slender girl; she'd hardly any waist to speak of. Some of her heavier colleagues had a terrible time with the tight garments. She took as deep a breath as she could, glancing down at herself to judge the effect. She hadn't much chest either, not compared to some of the lasses, but what there was had been pushed up and out in a way she knew to be enticing.

This dress was the most expensive thing she owned. Red satin, bright as fresh blood, underlay a web of fine black lace. The cut was scandalously low and the skirt just high enough to hint at her well-turned ankles. Her hair, long and wavy, was carefully and deliberately disheveled, leaving loose auburn curls wandering down her girlish cheeks. Those cheeks were rouged, her lips tinted a shocking crimson.

She looked, in short, precisely the sort of girl any respectable lady would avoid—and any respectable gentleman would avoid during daylight hours. But after nightfall it was a different song and the gentlemen danced to a darker tune, wandering the cobblestones in search of night flowers to pluck. Coventry appeared to be just such a flower, watching and waiting.

She had to be careful. Whitechapel was no place to forget oneself. She knew, better than most, what sort of men lurked thereabouts. And unlike most of the girls, she had no stout fellow to look after her interests. Coventry Adams worked only for herself, so she'd learned to keep her wits about her.

A pair of horses clop-clopped along the lane to her front. Her keen ear caught the difference at once. These were no plodding cart-horses. This was a carriage team, perfectly matched in size and stride, high-stepping and proud. She heard the creak of springs just behind them and knew they were pulling a gentleman's coach. Not only that, it was moving slowly. That could mean only one thing. Toffs would scarcely linger in such a neighborhood, not unless they were looking for something.

This gentleman was either engaged in some other unsavory business, or he was on the lookout for a girl like her.

Coventry had seen what happened to pedestrians who stumbled in front of carriages. The heavy wheels could crack skulls and shatter bones. She eased forward, taking care to keep her feet up on the curb, but making herself noticeable. She took two paces to her right, so the light of the nearest lamp shone down on her face and décolletage. And she waited.

The coach emerged from the fog scant seconds later, a fine double brougham, drawn by two beautiful coal-black Friesians. The carriage itself was finely ornamented, sporting a coat of arms on the door, though it was impossible to make out in the misty night.

Coventry waited until the carriage was in the act of passing her by. Then she cast a coy glance over her shoulder. She couldn't see into the darkened interior, of course, but that was not the point. The point was to display herself to the best possible effect, mingling false modesty with the promise of dark delights.

The carriage went only a few paces further. Then it came to a halt as the driver, in answer to some signal from within, pulled the horses up short. The animals stood, champing their bits, the mist of their breath mingling with the fog.

The coachman stood, a towering, shadowy figure in a heavy overcoat and wide-brimmed hat. He jumped down to the cobblestones, but even then, he overtopped Coventry by nearly a foot. She had learned through bitter experience to watch a man's hands. His held a riding whip. A lash from it might sting, but it was hardly a proper weapon. A cudgel or sword would have been worse. Still, Coventry tensed to run. She knew the alley at her back, every twist and turn of it. Give her half a breath's start and she would be gone.

The coachman opened the brougham's door and stood back, respectful.

"My dear young girl, whatever are you doing out so late, in such a dreadful place?"

The voice that came out of the darkened coach was a round, deep, jovial sort of voice, one that could only come from a fat, well-fed belly. It was a voice a frightened girl might run to for comfort. Coventry did not trust it one bit.

"Please, guv'nor," she said, laying on a strong Cockney accent. "It is so terribly late, and here's myself, all out on my own. I don't suppose you'd know where I might find a place to stay, maybe to lay down for a bit?"

"Oh, you poor dear thing," the man said. "And just look at you, dreadfully exposed to the cold. You must be simply shivering! Why don't you climb up here and get warm, out of the night air?"

It was the usual dance. Some of the girls laughed at such preliminaries, considering them a waste of valuable time. But Coventry knew better. Rituals were important. They put men at ease. And men at their ease were men off their guard.

"Oh, thanks ever so much, guv," she said. "If you could just give me a hand?" She raised one hand, clad in a black, elbow-length glove. Her other hand stayed at her side, near a hidden pocket she'd sewn into her dress. Inside that pocket lay a long, slim blade of forged steel, about the size of a knitting needle but sharpened along both edges. One never could tell with gentleman callers, especially those who liked their girls young.

A large, beefy hand enclosed her slender fingers. She put her foot on the step and hoisted herself up into the carriage. The coachman immediately closed the door behind her. Coventry felt a momentary thrill of fear. She embraced it, letting the fear strip years off her voice and demeanor. Genuine fear was much more convincing than any counterfeit. She was nineteen, but could pass for fifteen or twenty-five, as circumstances required. She had the feeling this man would like her to be very young indeed.

"This is awful kind of you, guv," she said.

"Not at all, dear girl, not at all," he said cheerfully. In the shadows, his face was still hard to make out, but Coventry was nearly overcome by a sudden, dizzy feeling of familiarity. She was glad of the darkness. She knew this man, or had known him, years ago. Would he remember?

Not bloody likely, she thought. That had been a very different time and place. She forced down memories of long ago: a big house in the country, dinner parties, fashionable events, hunts and picnics. But his name came to her unbidden. Bartleby Horrocks, Minister of Parliament. What had he been worth? Seventy thousand pounds a year?

Coventry smothered a smile. This was a real toff, a man with wealth and position, stooping to demean himself with a sweet young night flower. She was going to enjoy this.

"My darling girl," he said, still dancing the familiar steps, though they both knew the inevitable outcome. "I shall be only too delighted to place myself at your service. I am merely a visitor in London, but if I might prevail upon you to accompany me to my hotel, you might find such... ah... repose and refreshment as the hour allows."

This was better than she had allowed herself to hope. Her fear had been he might just want a quick tumble in the carriage. That would force her hand and would require speed and risky action, particularly if she was forced to deal with the coachman as well. But to go to his room was far preferable. It should afford plenty of more leisurely opportunities amidst greater security and comfort.

"Cor, guv, that's lovely," she said, placing a hand on his knee and nestling in close beside him. "I just knew some kind gentleman such as yourself would find me."

He put an arm around her shoulder in a gesture that should have been paternal and comforting but was neither. Coventry felt the trembling hunger in his touch. She cared not a toss. Her close proximity had already told her he had a gold pocketwatch in his silk waistcoat, and she was fair certain in which pocket his pocketbook resided.

This looked to be a very profitable night.

Keeping Mr. Horrocks's advances at bay during the carriage ride presented no great difficulty. Coventry was an old hand at promising without delivering. She remembered her early classical education. The myth of Tantalus, in particular, was applicable to her trade. The trick was to offer just enough to set the hook. Then a girl could play a man like a fish on a line, letting him wriggle and exhaust himself. The difficulty was, in the end one had to either land the fish or cut the line, and it was sometimes hard to know which.

Bartleby Horrocks, however, was an amateur in such matters. Coventry's touch set him all aflutter while holding him off. Men were all the same, aiming for the destination with no thought of the journey. Coventry took a certain pride in convincing them to stop and take in the sights along the way.

By the time the carriage stopped outside the hotel, Mr. Horrocks was so much quivering putty in her skillful hands. Now was the time to conclude negotiations. A few whispered words, delivered alongside the delicate application of the tip of her tongue to his earlobe, convinced Mr. Horrocks she was worth a half-crown at the least. Some of the girls were content to settle for a hay-penny knee-trembler in a back alley. Coventry aimed higher. She had learned that a higher price, rather than putting off a would-be purchaser, actually commanded respect, even admiration.

With their bargain amicably struck, Coventry and Mr. Horrocks alighted from the carriage. The driver assisted Mr. Horrocks with his considerable bulk, while Mr. Horrocks gallantly offered a hand to Coventry. The hotel doorman looked askance at them as they approached.

"Your pardon, sir," he said. "Who is this young... lady?"

"My niece," Mr. Horrocks said blandly.

"Your... niece," the doorman repeated, raising a very skeptical eyebrow and letting his eyes travel over Coventry's face and décolletage.

"Indeed," Mr. Horrocks said, passing his hand close to the footman's. There was a clink of coin as money changed hands.

"Yes, quite," the doorman said. "Welcome, sir. Madam."

So Coventry passed into a rather nice hotel on the arm of a respectable gentleman. Everyone knew what she was; her clothing and cosmetics trumpeted it. But no one raised an outcry. She might as well have been invisible, for all the notice anyone paid. She idly wondered, as they walked up a carpeted stairway, whether the doorman's bribe was more than what she had demanded to purchase what remained of her virtue. A shilling normally sufficed for such a man, but perhaps the rates had gone up of late.

Mr. Horrocks unlocked his door and ushered her in with a slight bow. Coventry replied with a half-curtsy.

"You, my dear, are quite remarkable," Mr. Horrocks said. "Truly a flower among the stones of Whitechapel."

"It's right kind of you to say, guv," she said, taking in the room at a glance. "Near poetry, that was." The chamber was impressive, if not quite palatial. Bartleby Horrocks was living in somewhat understated style at present. Did that signify he had fallen on hard times? It was so difficult to tell with gentlemen. They were quite skilled at keeping up appearances.

"Your speech marks you as a resident of London's, ah, lower quarter," Mr. Horrocks continued. "Yet your fresh and dewy complexion, the paleness of your skin, suggest otherwise. Might I inquire your name?"

"Everyone calls me Coventry, sir," she said. "Like the city."

"What a peculiar name for a lovely girl. Would you care for a drop of brandy, Miss Coventry?"

"That'd be lovely, guv. What ought I call you?"

"Mr. Hanover."

A lie, of course, but Coventry could hardly complain. After all, she was being no more honest than he. None of this was true, none of it was real.

"It's a pleasure, Mr. Hanover," she said, taking his hand. He lowered his lips and kissed her hand. Even through her glove, she could feel the hunger in his lips. His mouth was open, his breath hot and moist on her wrist. She suppressed a shudder, turning it to an eager quiver of her own, knowing it would be effective. Men saw what they wished to see.

Mr. Horrocks reluctantly released her hand and turned to a table on which stood a decanter and several glasses. As he filled two cups, Coventry slid a hand into another hidden pocket in her dress and extracted a little packet of powder. She held it neatly between her second and third fingers, hidden from view.

Mr. Horrocks turned, glasses in hand. Coventry started to reach for one, then feigned a stumble and caught at his arm with her left hand. He made a startled noise and nearly spilled the brandy. While he was thus distracted, she passed her opposite hand over the other glass, letting the powder spill from the little packet into the beverage.

"Sorry, guv," she gasped. "It's these wee shoes I'm wearing. They do squeeze my ankles so. I don't suppose you'd mind if I removed them?"

Mr. Horrocks was poleaxed by the thought of Coventry's dainty little feet and ankles clad in naught but stockings. In that distracted state, he certainly did not notice the powder dissolving into his brandy. One of the most important tricks in sleight-of-hand was drawing the mark's attention away at the perfect moment.

"Quite all right," he stammered.

"Thanks ever so, guv," she said, plucking the other glass from his hand. She wanted to savor it. After all, good brandy was hard to come by on the street. But the main thing was to make sure he drank, so she tossed back her glass in one gulp. It burned pleasantly on the way down, warming her insides marvelously. Mr. Horrocks, naturally, could not allow a young woman to outdo him in the imbibing of drink, so he followed suit. An odd expression crossed his face and he looked down at the glass.

"Rather bitter, that," he said thoughtfully. "I say, Miss Coventry, did yours taste a trifle off?"

"Don't know what you mean, guv," she said. "But if you're wanting another taste on your lips..."

She stepped in close, tilted her head up, and kissed him, letting him feel the whole length of her. She laid one hand on his cheek, the other against his chest, and nibbled lightly on his lower lip.

He groaned and closed his eyes. "Oh, my dear," he said. "You really are too much."

"You've no idea," she whispered, tugging him across the room toward the bedroom. He followed willingly enough. She helped him out of his jacket, hanging it on the back of a nearby chair. Then she turned him about so his back was to the bed and gave him a playful push. He stumbled backward. Then the mattress took him just behind the knees and he fell across a pillow with a soft whoosh.

"Fell over," he said, his words slurring together. "Most... curious..."

"Not to worry, guv," Coventry said. "You just need a wee lie-down is all. Just lie quiet and close your eyes, and I'll take care of the rest."

Mr. Horrocks obediently did so. Soon he was dreaming, a smile spread across his pudgy face.

Coventry gave the drug another minute to work, counting the seconds by the beat of her own pulse. Then she said quietly, "Mr. Hanover? Sir?"

He made no response.

She leaned in quite close and nipped his ear between her teeth, something sure to make any man jump. He lay perfectly still.

Nodding in satisfaction, Coventry set to work. The tincture of opium had been prepared by a Chinese fellow she knew, a man who ran a den by the docks that catered to sailors. She had used it before, and while its effects were somewhat unpredictable, she could count on at least thirty minutes before Mr. Horrocks returned to wakefulness. Undressing the unconscious man was the work of a few distasteful moments. In the process, she divested him of the gold wedding ring he really did not deserve to wear. She rifled his clothing, acquiring thereby his gold pocketwatch, his pocketbook, three crowns, two shillings, and thruppence in loose coin, and a pair of handsome diamond-stud cufflinks. Those were distinctive, and dangerous to sell, but too valuable to leave behind. The pocketbook was the real prize. A quick glance showed her it held banknotes, rather a lot of them.

Before leaving Mr. Horrocks to his opium-fueled dreams, she thoughtfully draped a sheet over him. It wouldn't do to have him catching cold, after all. His clothes were of fine make, but the resale of fabric was not really in Coventry's line, so she left them in a pile on the floor and turned her attention to the hotel room.

She knew better than to steal anything belonging to the hotel. Mr. Horrocks would be unlikely to report a theft, given the nature of the young woman who had come to his room. It would create awkward questions he would have no wish to answer. But if the hotel noticed anything of theirs missing, they would report it to the police. That was a risk not worth the taking.

She settled for pillaging Mr. Horrocks's personal baggage. The results were a fine silver shaving kit, another two pairs of cufflinks, a second pocketwatch—this one of silver—and a few interesting bits and bobs whose value she could not guess. But Fergie, the fellow who ran the rag and bottle shop, would give her a fair price for them. They went into the deep pockets in her skirt's lining, together with the rest of the loot.

Before leaving, she went to the washbasin and looked at herself in the mirror. Small details were important. One needed to show others what they expected to see. She tousled her hair and smeared her lipstick. She adjusted her dress to look as if it had been hastily rearranged. She splashed water in her eyes, making sure to leave trails on her cheeks like the ghosts of tears. Then she let herself out of the room.

She knew the trick of working locks with a pair of hairpins, but there seemed little point in locking the door, and it was a needless risk. She let it be and stumbled down the stairs, trailing one hand along the wall to support herself. It was all too easy to put the look on her face of a young girl who had just had something dreadful done to her.

The doorman looked at her coldly. He did not open the door for her.

"P-please, sir," she whimpered. "May I... may I go?"

His face softened slightly as he took in her state. Then his jaw tightened and his eyes went icy, but his anger was directed elsewhere.

"Bloody bastard," he muttered under his breath. "If he wasn't a blooming minister, I'd knock his teeth down his bloody throat." He held the door for her. "Sorry for your troubles, madam."

"Th-thank you, sir," Coventry stammered, even managing to fill her eyes with artificial tears. She felt a very slight twinge of guilt. He seemed a decent chap and it was a shame to play him that way. But it wasn't as if she was robbing him. He'd already done well out of the night's adventures, and she noted he made no effort to offer her the coins Mr. Horrocks had given him.

She held to the act all the way to the end of the street. Only once she had turned the corner and was safely enveloped in the fog did she stand upright again. Then, as she considered the long walk back to Whitechapel, a hansom cab appeared in front of her, an answer to her unspoken prayer.

It was an extravagance, surely, but one she could now afford, and it would save her a long and dangerous walk. Coventry raised a hand and waved to the driver. Some nights, one truly was blessed by fortune.

Chapter 2

Coventry took her usual precautions on the way to her bolt-hole, asking the cabbie to drop her a fair distance away, reversing direction several times, and crossing the street twice. Content that she was not being followed, she eased into an alley, up a rickety back stair, and into the foul smell and smoke of a gambling hall. She nodded a cheery greeting to Nick, the burly man who watched the door. She crossed the room, playfully slapping away the hands of a couple of the lads as she danced past them.

"You're in a right rare mood, Cov," Slinky McGee observed. "Good night?"

"Best of 'em, Slinky," she said, winking.

"If you're wanting, we could deal you in," he said. "Or you can sit on my lap and play my cards for me."

"You'd like that, you old goat," she said. "I may be just a wee scrap of a girl, but I'm more woman than the likes of you'll ever manage."

Slinky put his hand over his heart in mock distress. Coventry saw only smiles on familiar faces. She knew every man in the room. Society would consider them bad men, she supposed, but they were really decent enough chaps once one scraped away the surface dirt. She'd been rooming here nearly three months, longer than she'd rested in any one place in years, and she was starting to feel almost at home.

With a flirty wave to her admirers, she swirled her skirt and pranced down the back hall to her room, snatching up a candle as she went.

"You'll be paying for that bit of wax, love!" Slinky called after her.

"I'll toss an extra farthing in with my rent come Monday, you penny-pinching flapdoodle," she tossed over her shoulder.

She made certain to lock the door and shoot the bolt the moment she was inside. There was a difference between feeling at home and being a fool.

The room mightn't be much to look at, but by Whitechapel standards it was a right treat. To start with, it was hers and hers alone, with a real solid door. No mere ragged curtain separated her from a consumptive neighbor or a litter of squalling brats. The ceiling was sloped low on one side, so she could only stand upright near the door, but the place was furnished with a mattress stuffed with rags, only slightly verminous; a tub for laundry and bathing so she needn't go to the shared washroom; and a few pegs for her clothes. There was even a small, grimy window with all its panes intact. In spite of the cold, it was propped open a hands-breadth.

"Whisper?" she called quietly.

After a brief, breathless pause, a faint *meow* answered her.

"There you are, you precious wee thing," Coventry said, kneeling down and extending a hand. A rangy black cat materialized out of the shadows in the corner of the room, green eyes glowing in the candlelight. Whisper stalked slowly to meet the girl, sniffed her hand, and rubbed his cheek against her knuckles.

Coventry stroked the cat's neck and back. "I've not brought you anything," she said. "But I promise we'll take a stroll down to the market tomorrow and find some fresh fish. I've had a brilliant night and we'll not be wanting for vittles today, nor tomorrow, and who's to say fairer than that?"

Whisper purred, his tail rising at every stroke of her hand.

Now that she knew the cat was in for the night, Coventry closed the window. Whisper got in and out that way, running across the rooftops as easily as the lads came and went by door and stair. He was hardly her cat. It was fairer to say, she was his girl. He'd announced himself the first night she'd spent in this place, proving that the room was not quite unoccupied, despite Slinky's promise. The two of them got on famously. Coventry left the window ajar for him, no matter the cold, and gave him little tidbits as occasion and income allowed. In return, Whisper kept the room free of rats and mice and provided a warm, undemanding bed-mate.

Coventry pried up a loose floorboard under a corner of her mattress, revealing the little hiding-place she'd worked out for herself. She took out the loot she'd pilfered from Mr. Horrocks and gave it a quick once-over, then deposited it in the hole and replaced the board. The banknotes were the best, of course, but the very size of the denominations promised to be difficult to dispose of. Perhaps they'd be best as a nest egg, something to save for a rainy day. But she'd do well to sell the traceable goods to Fergie as quick as she could, come morning.

She took off her red dress, stripping down to her chemise and sighing with relief once she'd rid herself of the corset. Then, already shivering a little with the cold, she pulled on her plain, ragged nightgown and rolled herself in her woolen blanket. Her pillow was a bundle of rags, faintly moldy but really not bad, and she shared the bed with only a few fleas. On the whole, things could be a great deal worse.

Whisper curled in beside her. Coventry put an arm around the cat, bundling him close, enjoying the throaty rumble of his contented purring. Soon both were asleep.

The fog had lifted and the sun was well up by the time Coventry reluctantly abandoned the nest of warmth she and Whisper had made for themselves. The London sky was barely visible through the grimy window, clouds of coal-smoke from the chimneys blotting out the blue. Still, it didn't look likely to rain, and that was something to be thankful for.

While Whisper luxuriously stretched and saw to his morning toilet, daintily licking his paws and running them over his head, Coventry washed her own face, using a polished tin plate for a mirror. She made certain to remove all trace of her tart's makeup. What was left was a young woman who could pass for a girl. She sometimes cursed her fresh face and wide, innocent blue eyes. If she'd not been such a looker, she'd not likely have come to this pass. Still, once the gin was spilt in the gutter, there was precious little use crying over it. She put on her other dress, her everyday dress. This was pale blue, stained a bit at the hem, darkened with coal-dust, and starting to fray at the cuffs. And, of course, it went over the thrice-damned corset and crinoline cage.

Inside a quarter of an hour, her hair tucked back in a braid, looped and pinned around her head, Coventry looked like any young woman of modest means and good character. She had a wicker shopping-basket to hold on her arm and a plain narrow-brimmed hat that matched the dress. Unable to resist a small indulgence, she gave the hat a saucy tilt. In the bottom of the basket, under a folded cloth, were the jewelry and knickknacks formerly belonging to Bartleby Horrocks. Tucked up the right sleeve of the dress, clipped to her forearm, was her stiletto. Thus fortified, Coventry Adams emerged to meet the day.

She had gone only two paces down the hall when Whisper began frisking about her ankles. Apparently he thought it best to accompany her to market to protect his investment in her.

"As you will, you wee dark lump," she said with an affectionate smile. "But don't you come crying if a cart runs over that tail you're waving so proud."

Whisper looked up at her and blinked as if to suggest he was affronted by the mere suggestion of such clumsiness.

Daylight revealed, in unflinching clarity, all the dingy ugliness of Whitechapel. The name, Coventry thought, had never suited the neighborhood. The colors of Whitechapel were dirty brick and dingy grey. Not even the linens on the clotheslines were white, not once the coal-smoke got to them. When she'd been a girl, Coventry had read about the peppered moths in one of her father's books. In 1811, the moths had been white with dark grey spots. Less than forty years later, a field collection in Manchester had revealed they were being rapidly replaced by their cousins, black-bodied with wings the color of soot.

The Darwinians, of course, had seized on this as evidence of their radical theory of natural selection. Coventry took a more practical lesson to heart. If one wanted to survive in a dark world, one had best learn how to blend with the shadows.

How she missed books! She dreamed, sometimes, of her father's library. To have a whole room devoted to nothing but the storage of knowledge! It was a silly, girlish dream, she knew, but sometimes she wept for it.

But dreams and tears were for lonely nights of slumber. Now that she was awake, she had best keep her wits about her. The air was sharp and cold, the wind whipping color into her cheeks. She glided through the crowds, avoiding contact whenever possible, forcing a path when she must. She was small, but she knew how to command her space, to project herself into her environs. And she had a knack with words, particularly the vicious abuse the fishwives slung about the market. Coventry could fair blister the ears of even the most debauched rowdy.

Her first stop this day was Fergie's rag and bottle shop, a dilapidated little store a stone's throw from the market. She pushed the door open, hearing the tinkle of the little bell that hung from the ceiling, and stepped into the dark interior. Whisper scuttled in on her heels.

The shop was very dark, for the windows were so dusty they might as well have been bricked up. Sagging shelves groaned and creaked under the weight of countless piles of worthless detritus. The place was a veritable maze, but Coventry had been here many times before and knew her way about. She walked confidently along the serpentine path that led to the counter, catching a glimpse of a skittering little creature out of the corner of her eye.

Whisper saw it too. The cat crouched, tail lashing. Then he pounced, a brief scuffle and a muffled squeak heralding the end of the mouse's short, sad life. Whisper rejoined Coventry, tail waving like a triumphant flag, a limp grey body dangling from his mouth.

"Fergie!" Coventry called.

"That you, Cov?" called a reedy Irish-accented voice.

"Now who else would I bloomin' well be?" she retorted. She had reached the counter, which was likewise piled with junk, but saw no sign of the proprietor.

"Can't be too careful," Fergie replied, popping into view like a jack-in-the-box. He was an odd-looking little man, all skinny limbs and bony joints, tufts of hair thrusting haphazardly from all points of his skull. He grinned lopsidedly when he saw her. His whole face was slightly off-kilter, which made one want to tilt one's head when looking at him to find an angle from which he looked right.

"Got something I thought you'd want a butcher's at," she said. It had taken her some time, when she had first landed on the streets, to catch the knack of the Cockney rhyming slang. In this case, "butcher's" was short for "butcher's hook," rhyming with "look," which was what she was actually saying. It was an almost impenetrable dialect, which was precisely the point. Cockneys had no interest in speaking clearly to outsiders. Knowing the slang was a shibboleth, a gateway to lower-class London.

"Well, let's have a gander," Fergie said. "Always a pleasure to see you, Cov. You're looking lovely as ever."

Coventry, after a quick look over her shoulder to ensure they were alone, spread out her offerings on a small space of open countertop. She'd have done better to deal the items singly, to specialists; she knew a horologist who'd pay good money for the watches, to begin with. But she wanted to be rid of Horrocks's knickknacks quickly. It was an intuition, a twinge in her innards, without anything to reinforce it, but a street girl quickly learned to pay attention to such hunches.

Fergie fumbled in his pocket for an eyeglass. He screwed it into his right eye, making his face even more lopsided than before. He picked up the items one by one and squinted at them.

How the fence could see anything in this light was a mystery to Coventry. Perhaps he never went outside, and so remained acclimated to the shadows. Certainly she had never seen him anywhere but this shop. Whisper might have better night-vision than Fergie, but she would place no wager on it.

"Hmm, very nice, very nice," Fergie murmured. Some fences pretended disinterest in their wares, figuring to drive a cheaper bargain, but Fergie valued his long-running relationship with Coventry. He knew if he tried to skin her, he might get away with it once, but if she found out, she'd take her business elsewhere in the future. Besides, Coventry had a better eye for jewelry than many street girls and would be hard to cheat.

"I'm guessing you didn't buy these from Asprey or Garrard," he said, speaking of two of the posher jewelers in London.

"Got them off a gentleman," she said with a bland smile.

"Presents, were they?"

"Not precisely."

Fergie nodded. He didn't need to know the details, nor did he wish to. He only needed to know whether the articles were stolen. Coventry had just told him that, though not in so many words.

"I'll give you fifty quid for the lot," he said.

"You'll sell them for five hundred," she said. "I'll be wanting a hundred of that."

"They're fair scorching," he argued. "I'll not get anything close to market price. Sixty, and that's taking bread out of the mouths of my wee ones."

"If you're a father, I'm the Archbishop of bloody Canterbury," she retorted. "Eighty and they're yours."

"Enough haggling," he said. "We both know you'll settle for sixty-five."

"Don't be putting words in my mouth, when what we both know is we'll meet at seventy-five."

"Done." Fergie grinned and offered his hand. Coventry shook with him, almost managing to avoid thinking about where his hand might have been or what it might have been doing. "Half a moment, I'll fetch your coin."

He bustled into his back room and returned a few moments later with a cigar-box that rattled enticingly. He opened the box so the lid was between them and counted out an odd collection of well-worn coinage. Coventry didn't mind the blackened shillings and clipped guineas. Old coins raised no eyebrows and would be easy to spend.

"Be seeing you, Fergie," she said. "This world or a better."

"If you wind up in heaven, you'll be waiting a long time for me," he cackled, ending in a dusty coughing fit. "Mind your step, Cov, and don't take too many chances. I know you're a dab hand, but a hundred brilliant jobs won't make up for the one you botch."

Back on the street again, Whisper still proudly carrying his kill, she and the cat made their way to the market. There Coventry bought a loaf of bread, a wedge of cheese, two bottles of cheap red wine, two cabbages, and some salt beef. True to her word, she then went to the fishmongers to see about a nice tidbit for Whisper.

The fishwives were the best gossips in the market. Coventry always put her ear to the ground when she visited. One never knew when one might hear something of interest, or of possible value. As she perused the day's catch, she heard one of the women reading from the newspaper. Few of these women had mastered their letters, so a knot of them had clustered around the reader, hungry for news.

"...found *murdered* in his hotel room," the woman was saying, sounding out the critical word with morbid delight.

"Murdered?" one of the listeners echoed, to the accompaniment of a chorus of theatrical gasps. Bloody violence was always good for a bit of entertainment.

"Just think of it!" another said. "Such a great man, too!"

"Hush!" a third said. "Go on, Nora, tell us what it says!"

"Au-thor-i-tees are in-ves-ti-ga-ting," Nora said, getting over the long words with difficulty. "They suspect the victim had an... an..."

"Yes?" several breathless voices asked.

But the word "assignation" was beyond Nora's literary grasp. "He was entertaining a tart in his room," she said, guessing at the meaning.

Heads bobbed knowingly. Even the toffs were only human, after all. Serve him right if he was done in by one of those women. But the thought of it was titillating, adding a bit of spice to an already sordid tale.

"The Met-ro-pol-i-tan Police expect to app-re-hend the mal-e-fac-tor quickly," Nora said. "Scotland Yard has placed one of its rising stars on the job."

"'Ere, Nora, what's a rising star?" a woman inquired.

"It means a lad who's not on top yet, but he'll get there," her companion explained.

"Detective Farrell declined to comment," Nora recited. "But this reporter is sure this grisly and brutal murder will not go long un-avenged, and Minister Horrocks will have justice."

All the blood drained out of Coventry's face. She told herself it was only the squeeze of her corset, but she could scarcely draw breath. She never fainted, never, but for a moment the fishmarket spun about her.

"'Ere, madam, you all right?"

A rough but friendly pair of hands caught her just under the shoulders. Coventry blinked and saw the mustached face of a fisherman. He had weather-beaten cheeks but bright eyes. Coventry had learned to pay close attention to what could be seen in a man's eyes. She saw nothing here but kindness and concern. His hands were carefully placed so as to give no offense.

"I'm all right," she said, trying to smile but managing only to look sickly. "Just got taken a bit funny is all."

"Sit down for a spell," he suggested, gesturing to a nearby wooden crate. "You'll feel better in a bit."

"No, thank you, sir," she said, waving him off. "I... I must be going."

She extricated herself from her would-be helper and fled the market. Her head was awhirl with horror. *Dear God,* she thought. *Bartleby Horrocks, dead? The opium? Surely not!*

But opium had killed many a healthy lad before Mr. Horrocks. What if she had administered too much of the stuff? What if the mixture had been bad? Good Lord, she had killed the poor man! Granted, he was a filthy womanizing beast, but *murder?*

She was a murderer. The full force of law and society would be turned against her, determined to run her to earth like a fox. Then a trial, prison, and… and the gallows. But that was not the worst of it. Coventry Adams had sworn never to take a human life, no matter the reason. And now, for the sake of a few pretty trinkets, she had lost all that was left of her soul. She would die and burn in Hell.

She fled almost blindly, rushing she knew not where, hot tears burning in her eyes. She thrust through crowds of Londoners, heedless of their indignant cries, possessing neither plan nor direction. Where could she go? What could she do? She had nothing, no one. She was utterly lost.

Panic was well enough, in its way, while it lasted. But sooner or later, sanity always prevailed. Coventry's wits drifted back after perhaps half an hour. She had been weeping, to judge from her red and swollen eyes. Her feet, punished by the cobblestones, ached. So did her head. She did not immediately know where she was.

As her fear subsided a little, anger flooded in to replace it. She was angry principally with herself. She knew better than to rush off like some little fool, headlong into whatever dangers might surround her. There would be time enough later to punish herself for what she had done. For now, she had to think.

"Go back," she whispered to herself. "Fetch your bits of things. Then away." A ship, perhaps. Across the Channel to France? That might serve. She knew enough French to get on with. A new city would be dangerous, surely, but how much worse could it be?

She looked about her, taking in her surroundings, and quickly recognized the street. Even in her panic, she had been thinking better than she knew. She was only five minutes' walk from Slinky's gambling hall, and home.

An anxious meow, coupled with a furry pressure against her ankle, made her glance down. There was Whisper. He had dropped his mouse somewhere along the way, but he had kept near her. Now he stared up at her and cocked his head quizzically.

Coventry gulped at the sudden lump in her throat. She was not, after all, completely alone. The thought gave her more strength than she would have thought possible. She still had her basket on her arm, containing the food she had bought. She had the money from Fergie hidden in her dress, and a great deal more under the floorboards. It was a slight risk, going back to fetch it, but one worth taking. She'd worked hard for that bit of scratch, and she'd need it, either to lie low in London or to travel.

She hurried, not quite running, into the familiar alley and up the stairs. Slinky's establishment was deserted at this early hour. Slinky himself was probably still asleep. She unlocked her room, went in, and gathered up her things. She nearly left the red satin dress behind. It had been expensive, but it was bulky. Nonetheless, after a moment's thought, she folded it as best she could into her one piece of luggage, a battered portmanteau almost too large for her. She ate a few quick bites of food, thrust the remainder of the bread, cheese, and beef into the suitcase, and took her leave, dropping a few coins on the mattress to pay her rent. She might be a thief, but she would never cheat her landlord. Slinky had always played straight with her and had been a decent friend. She laid the key beside the coins. The door she'd leave unlocked.

"Well, lad?" she asked Whisper. "Is this goodbye? If you're wanting to keep to your cove, good luck to you. I can't promise much, but I'll miss you."

The cat licked a paw and brushed it over one of his ears. Then, seeing Coventry stepping out of the room, suitcase in hand, he meowed and trotted to join her.

Coventry closed the door to Slinky's place behind her and started down the steps, wrestling with the portmanteau. She was thinking what dock to make for, and what time the next ship might sail. Her plans were falling into place. At the back of her mind, shock and dismay still clamored for her attention, but she ignored those emotions. *Time enough later*, she thought.

"Carry that for you, lass?"

The voice was young and pleasant, with the unmistakable lilt of Ireland. That was no surprise. The Irish were common enough in Whitechapel.

"No fear, lad," she replied. "I've got it." There wasn't a chance she'd trust her luggage to a complete stranger.

"A hand, then," he said as she neared the bottom of the stairs.

Coventry looked him over. He was only a few years older than she and quite a looker. His hair was dark and wavy, his mustache well-trimmed, his smooth cheeks showing he had managed to escape smallpox. He was dressed as a workingman, but something in his clothes looked just a trifle wrong. He held out a hand to assist her down the last few steps, smiling in a friendly fashion.

"And who'd you be, then?" she challenged.

"My mum called me Finbar," he said. "But most folk call me Finn. How's about you, madam?"

She hesitated. Her instincts, clouded by the emotional upheaval of the past moments, cried a sudden warning. The young man's eyes were a remarkable dark blue, very intense. She saw no cruelty in them, but she did see grim purpose.

"What's your business here, Finn?" she asked, putting her back against the alley wall and starting to sidle past him. She was suddenly, terribly afraid.

"I'm hoping to find a wee lass," he said. "I've heard she stays hereabouts. A bonnie colleen, so they say, quite young, reddish-brown hair. Looks a fair bit like yourself, come to that."

Too late, Coventry identified him. *Copper*, she thought, and with that one word she panicked again. Dropping her portmanteau, she spun on her heel and started for the alley entrance.

Coventry was fast, but Finn was too swift for her. He had anticipated her flight. Before she had gone more than three running paces he was on her, gripping her wrist with a terribly strong hand. Coventry twisted, instinctively fighting the trap.

He had her right hand in his grasp, the one with the stiletto. She clawed at his face with her left, gouging at his eyes.

He turned his head aside, her nails raking his cheek. He seized her other wrist, holding both hands. Coventry kicked at his shin, then stomped on his foot, grinding down with her heel. Finn flinched but did not let go. She thrashed wildly, trying to drive her forehead into his face to break his nose, but he was clearly no stranger to street brawls and drew back out of her reach. He forced her hands down and spun her about, twisting her right arm up behind her back and slamming her into the brickwork.

The breath left her in a gasp, but Coventry still tried to fight. The feel of his body against her back called up awful memories of sordid alleyway trysts. She struggled wildly, desperately. But she was no match for his size and strength. He kicked her feet apart, making her totter. Then she felt cold steel against her skin, heard the clink of an adjustable wrist-bar.

"Forgive me," Finn said through clenched teeth. "I'd hoped not to need these, but you're giving me no choice, you wee wildcat." By his strained tone, she knew she'd caused him considerable pain, at least.

Her left hand was free for a second. Coventry squirmed frantically, but her case was hopeless. She was no match for his strength. Soon that hand, too, was pinioned behind her back, the cuffs clicking shut.

"Now," Finn said. "Let's step inside and catch our breath, shall we? I think we've a few things to discuss, you and I."

Chapter 3

Numbly, Coventry let Finn lead her back upstairs to the gambling hall. Finn guided her with one hand on her cuffs, carrying her suitcase in the other. Whisper had vanished as soon as the fight had started, sliding away like a blob of quicksilver. He was too canny an alley-cat to hang about once fists and feet began to fly.

Slinky McGee stood in the doorway, mouth hanging open. He'd heard the commotion and arrived just in time to witness its end.

"Here now, guv," he said to the Irishman. "What's all this?"

"Detective Finbar Farrell, Metropolitan Police," Finn said. "Doing my civic duty, sir. If you'd be so kind as to lend me the use of your fine establishment for the space of a few minutes, I'd be obliged."

Slinky's face darkened and he gave the inspector an unfriendly look. "How do I know you're a detective?" he demanded.

Finn opened his coat, showing the gleam of a white metal badge and the handle of a stout truncheon. "Here's my authority," he said. "If the badge won't suffice, I'm thinking my shillelagh will."

Slinky held up his hands, palms outward, and retreated indoors. Finn steered Coventry in behind him and sat her down at one of the tables. She offered no resistance. After the reflexive attempt at flight, she had collapsed in on herself. Perhaps she deserved to be caught, she thought bitterly. She had betrayed her last principles. She truly was nothing now, deserving neither mercy nor forgiveness.

"Now then," Finn said, taking out a notebook and a little nub of a pencil. "Let's start with your name, shall we?"

She made no answer.

"Come now, lass," Finn said. "Surely that much will do no harm, aye?" His voice was surprisingly gentle, and he showed no anger, though he now sported a swelling under one eye and blood trickled down his cheek where her nails had raked him.

"What's in a name?" Coventry retorted. "You calls it a rose, but it's still got bloody thorns on it, don't it?"

Finn's smile showed straight, white teeth; a rarity in Whitechapel. "That's not precisely how I've heard it said, but near enough. Round the public houses hereabouts, I've heard the name Coventry. Coventry Adams. Have I heard right?"

"You tell me, you bloody great mutton shunter. You've naught better to do than hassle working girls, so I guess you ought to know."

Finn raised an eyebrow. "You're misinformed, lass," he said. "I've never been on that particular detail. I fear my work's a mite more serious than chasing tarts off street-corners. I'm tasked with investigating the murder of the honorable Bartleby Horrocks."

"Honorable, was he?" Coventry snorted. She was trying to rebuild some semblance of defiance, but she knew it was no use.

She could feel her lip quivering, could feel the tears trying to spring up again.

"It's a title, not a character reference," Finn said. "Be that as it may, he was found murdered in his bed in the wee hours. One of the hotel's other guests reported hearing a disturbance in his suite. A young woman clad in red was seen both entering and leaving the hotel. She entered in his company and departed a short while later on her own, disheveled and visibly distressed. The woman in question was described as some eighteen years of age, reddish brown hair, pale skin, unusually pretty."

Coventry bit her lip to still its quivering and stared into Finn's midnight-blue eyes, searching for hope, for some escape from this nightmare.

"Upon speaking with the late Mr. Horrocks's driver, I discovered the neighborhood in which the mysterious woman had been taken up," Finn went on. "This approximately matched the area of Whitechapel in which a cabbie deposited a woman, identical in appearance, later that night. I made discreet inquiries, dropping a few coins in public houses, and learned the lass's name and occupation. She calls herself Coventry Adams and passes as a lady of, shall we say, negotiable affection."

"I'm no bloody tart," Coventry spat. "Not anymore."

"Nay, that's true enough," Finn said. "My understanding is, you make your living posing as a wagtail, but you're really more of a pickpocket, a roller, and a hornswoggler, aye?"

"You're bloody well-informed," she said. "I've no idea what you're talking to me for. Sounds like you've got it all figured, you damned clever-boots."

Finn leaned forward. "I want to know why, Coventry Adams," he said softly. "Why'd you kill him? It looks bad for you, I'll grant, but you're young and just a wee lass. He was a great fat jollocks of a lad who could scarce fit through a doorway. Did he hurt you? Did he misinterpret something you said and try to take advantage? Did he ravish you? What happened?"

"If I was a Papist, I'd confess to my priest," she said. "But you're no clergyman and I'm no bloody Catholic."

"I'm a member of the Catholic Church," Finn said placidly, rattling her portmanteau. "If I open this, might I be finding a red satin dress inside it?"

She said nothing.

"What about a knife?" he pressed. "I'm not surprised a lass would want one for protection. Do you carry a knife, Coventry?"

"I didn't mean to kill him," she blurted out. Something seemed to break within her. She began to weep, despising herself for weakness but unable to stop. Remorse was filling her to overflowing.

Finn nodded understandingly and made a note on his pad. "I'm certain you didn't," he said.

"I just needed him to lie quiet," she said, and now the tears were definitely flowing. "I couldn't have him pawing at me. I just needed a few minutes and to get out."

"It was robbery, then," Finn said. "You were after his money, aye?"

She nodded. "But he wasn't supposed to die. I'd never... never k-k-kill a man. Not... not on..." She tried to bury her head in her hands, but they were still cuffed behind her. She bowed her head and started to sob.

"Here now, lass, no need for that," Finn said. He produced a pocket handkerchief, plain but clean, and gently dabbed at her eyes. "Lads can be beastly to women, Lord knows I've seen it often enough. I've only been a detective these few months, but I walked my beat before that, and I know what men can do. It'll be all right. Now, I'm just needing the knife. Did you keep it?"

"Knife?" Coventry repeated dully.

"Aye, the knife," he said. "The one you stabbed him with."

"I never did," she said, confused. "What are you talking about?"

It was Finn's turn to look confused. "You told me you didn't mean to kill him," he said. "You were there. He stripped off his clothes, and likely tried to disrobe you as well. He came at you and you stabbed him. Four times." He indicated his chest with his index finger, poking it into himself at three points and finishing by jabbing himself under the chin.

Coventry shook her head, slowly at first, then more emphatically. "That's not what happened," she said.

"So now you're telling me you weren't there?" Finn's eyes grew still darker and more intense. The compassion was fading from them, replaced by the stern gaze of the Law.

"No! I was in the room! But I never stabbed him!"

"Where's your knife, Coventry?"

"I didn't... I don't..." she stammered.

Finn hefted her suitcase onto the table and flipped the catches, opening the lid. He began rifling through her belongings with quick, experienced hands.

Coventry's mind was racing. If Mr. Horrocks had been stabbed, then someone else had been in the room after she had left. Someone else had killed him. She was not the person for whom Finn sought. But like a bloody idiot, she had already confessed to having been there. Now the detective would never believe she she'd not done the deed. Once he'd finished with her baggage, he'd search her person. The moment he found the knife up her sleeve, it would be all over for her. She'd have a short future terminating at the gallows.

But the knowledge of her innocence had kindled new determination in Coventry. She sagged back in her chair, tilting her head to point her face toward the ceiling. In the process, she lowered the back of her skull toward her cuffed hands. By flexing her elbows, she was just able to reach her braid where it twined around her head. With her fingertips, she extracted one of her hairpins, then another.

"You made a tidy job of it," Finn observed, smoothing out her red dress and examining it. "I'm not seeing any bloodstains on the satin, though I warrant they'd be hard to spot against this color. Done this before, have you?"

"I never!" she snarled indignantly. Best to keep him talking and looking for clues. Behind her back, working by feel, she eased the first pin into the keyhole at her left wrist.

"Ah, no wonder you're feeling it, then," he said. "They say the first one's the hardest. But you needn't fret, lass. If you can give extenuating circumstances, it's possible the court may decide on transportation instead of the gallows, especially given your tender years. How old are you, lass?"

"Seventeen," she lied, fingers still working furiously. She had the second pin in place now and was trying to turn the tumblers. Handcuffs had simple locks, no real challenge, but when she had to work practically one-handed, behind her own back, all while doing her best not to jangle the chains, it was taking all her skill as a picklock.

He nodded sympathetically. "I'm a mite young for a detective myself," he confided. "Just twenty-five. But we do the work we've a knack for, aye? I think it's likely you'll be for Australia. You can make a new start there, find a good lad in need of a wife. It'll be a clean start of a sort. Now what else have we here?"

He took out the food and laid it on the table. He opened her cosmetic case and looked over the powders and paints. Coventry felt a slight shift in the cuffs. She feigned another sob to cover the click of the lock as it fell open. Her right wrist was still encased in its manacle, but her left hand was now free.

"I didn't kill Mr. Horrocks," she said, meeting Finn's eye. "I'm a thief, I'm a fallen woman, a bloody painted Jezebel, but I'm no damned murderer. Do you believe me?"

"It doesn't much matter what I believe," he said. "You'll have your chance to tell your story at trial. I'm not finding a weapon here, Coventry. I should've searched you first, and done a thorough job of it. I hope you'll forgive me taking liberties with your person. Have you a knife on you, by chance?"

He started to stand up, reaching toward her. It was now or never. Coventry sprang to her feet, grabbed the edge of the table, and tilted it. The table fell with a crash between the two of them, spilling all her worldly possessions across the floor of Slinky's gambling hall. Then she ran, but not for the exit. He'd be expecting that. She made for her old room, running the opposite direction.

Finn was surprisingly quick and nimble. He recovered from his surprise, dodged around the table, and came on fast. She had only the smallest of leads, but it sufficed to get her through the door three strides ahead of him. She slammed it in his face.

Coventry lunged for her mattress and came up with the key. She and Finn hit the door simultaneously. His greater bulk forced her back a pace and his hand came around the door. She saw his fingers right in front of her face.

With her left hand, she thrust the key into the lock. At the same moment, she swung her right arm against the door. The loose iron manacle, still shackled to her wrist, struck Finn square on the knuckles.

He let go of the door with an oath. Coventry rammed her shoulder against it and the door closed. She twisted the key, engaging the lock. Then she set her back against the wood planks and drew a few quick breaths.

"You've nowhere to run, Coventry," Finn said grimly. "You're only making this worse on yourself."

"I didn't kill him!" she snapped. "If you won't believe me, I'll find someone who bloody well does!"

"You'll have your day in court," he promised. "But the harder you fight, the worse things will go. My patience is wearing a bit thin, lass."

A heavy impact jarred against the door as he kicked it. The wood was flimsy and would not hold for long. Already one of the boards was cracking. The lock was cheap and might give way at any moment.

Coventry reached down and picked up the water-jug. She judged the distance and hurled it, end over end. The heavy pewter vessel went through the window with a splintering crash. Coventry followed it. A shard of broken glass scored her arm as she went through, another tore at her dress on the other side. It was a squeeze to get through the tiny garret window, but she was slender and she managed it.

As she braced herself on the slope of the roof and pulled her legs the rest of the way through, Finn delivered another mighty kick to the door and it gave way. She caught a glimpse of him rushing across the room, but she was already out and the window was too small for him. His shoulders were too broad.

They stared at one another for a moment, the girl just out of the detective's reach. The look in Finn's eyes now was reluctant admiration. He was actually smiling slightly.

"I didn't kill him," Coventry said for what felt like the tenth time.

"Then who did?" Finn asked.

"Damned if I know. I ought to ask you. You're the bloody detective."

"I'll chase you if you run," he said. "And I'll catch you."

She winked at him. "Promises, guv," she said, offering a saucy smile of her own. Then she turned away and started picking her way along the rooftop, holding her skirt free of her feet with one hand and bracing herself with the other.

Finn watched her a moment longer, shaking his head and chuckling softly. Then he left the window and ran out of the room.

Coventry knew she hadn't much time. Finn might not be able to reach her just then, but he knew exactly where she was. It was fortunate he apparently was not carrying a firearm. Most coppers were not issued guns, but enough of them carried the big Beaumont-Adams revolvers for her to be wary of them. Perhaps he did have one and simply had no wish to shoot down a fleeing woman. He did strike her as a chivalrous sort, particularly for a copper.

Her choices were to remain on the rooftops or to get down to street level. Both paths had advantages. As long as she stayed elevated, Finn would have to climb up to her. But true safety, such as it was, required her to descend sooner or later. He could summon more policemen and surround the row of houses. Then she'd be proper buggered. On the street, she might manage to lose herself in the crowds. But Finn was down there, along with God only knew how many more coppers. He might not have come alone.

She made her decision and started along the rooftops, making for the end of the row. The shingles were rotten and slippery and the going treacherous. She set one shoe on a particularly weak shingle and her foot plunged straight through. A startled cry came from the attic below.

"Sorry," Coventry said, jerking at her foot. It was a surprisingly difficult struggle to draw it back into the light. Her departure was hastened by a flood of invective from the inhabitant of the upper floor, who strongly objected to the ventilation of his roof. He'd be cursing her the next time it rained.

She climbed from one roof to the next, clutching the edge of a gable for support. As she went, she looked for a good way down. The distance was too great to chance a jump; if she so much as turned an ankle, her goose was truly cooked. But thus far, the only drainpipes she saw looked rusty and decidedly frail. She considered the edge of the roof. Just maybe, if she hung by her fingertips to shorten the distance, and aimed for a rubbish heap, she might make it without serious injury. Or she could chance breaking in through a gable window and making a run for it through whatever home lay below.

A familiar *meow* brought her up short.

"Whisper?" she said in surprise. There was the cat, perched nimbly on the next gable, staring with his eyes like green lamps.

How had the cat gotten up there? She marveled that she'd never considered it before. After all, in order to use her window, he must have a regular means of getting to the roof. But was it a path she could take?

"Go on, Whisper," she said, making a shooing motion with her hand.

He blinked lazily. Then, as if he had all the time in the world, the cat stretched luxuriously and trotted along the peak of the roof. Coventry watched him as he suddenly angled to his right, hopped easily to the top of another gable, and leapt out into space.

He landed nimbly atop a clothesline that slanted at a downward angle across the alley. It was a sturdy length of rope, more than sufficient to support the cat's weight. With the aplomb of a circus tightrope-walker, he pranced across and dropped to a little metal railing that ringed the window across the way. From there, he sprang down to the angled roof of a rickety shack someone had propped against the far wall. He slid down the roof and made three more quick hops down a pile of rubble to the alley.

"Nothing to it," Coventry muttered. "I just need to walk a blooming tightrope myself."

She wondered whether she was strong enough to go hand-over-hand across the alley and decided she was not. She was quick and agile, but not well-muscled in the arms. Most likely she'd make it halfway, then dangle helplessly until her fingers gave out and she fell, breaking her legs or her neck. She stood there, trying to think what to do. Precious seconds slipped away.

"Coventry Adams!"

"Oh bloody hell," she said under her breath. There was Finn, coming out onto the roof not more than twenty paces behind her. He'd opened a gable window from the inside and was crawling onto the rooftop. He was a quick one, no doubt of it. She backed toward the edge of the roof, keeping her eyes on him.

"You don't want to do that, lass," he said, breathing hard from his sprint and climb. "Just give me your hand and come in with me. We'll call it a day, aye?"

He extended a hand to her. It looked welcoming, but she knew what lay behind that hand: the courts, Newgate Prison, then the gallows at Tyburn or a transportation ship to Australia. She'd heard being transported was little better than being hanged, particularly for a young woman, no matter what Finn said.

"You're bloody persistent, Finn Farrell," she said.

He smiled slightly. "You don't know the half of it," he replied. "I'll not stop till I've got my hands on you."

"You know how many blokes have said the same?" she retorted, risking a quick look over her shoulder. Her heels were just at the very lip of the chasm. "I do seem to have that effect on most lads."

Finn advanced cautiously. He might be a dedicated copper, but he clearly had no wish to drag the both of them over the brink. "Help me and help yourself," he urged.

"One or t'other," she shot back. "Not both. You want me, Finn, you'll have to try a sight harder than that. Best prove your devotion, mate."

He had covered half the distance between them by now. He was still moving slowly, making sure of his footing. There was no rush; she clearly had nowhere to go.

Coventry suddenly crouched low, stooping over the clothesline where it was anchored to the wall. She tossed the empty bracelet of the handcuff over the line and grasped it with her free hand. Then she sucked in a quick breath and pushed off with both feet as hard as she could.

"Don't!" Finn shouted, but it was too late. Coventry felt a terrible jerk on her right wrist, the metal ring digging painfully into the base of her hand. She hung onto the other end of the cuffs for dear life. The chain whistled as she slid toward the opposite wall with increasing speed. She scarcely had time to swing her feet up and cushion herself. Her feet met the bricks with a jarring shock that traveled all the way up to her jaw. Her teeth clicked together hard, nearly snipping off the tip of her tongue.

Pressing herself flat against the wall, she felt down with her feet and found the railing beneath her. She let go of the chain and pulled herself free of the clothesline. As she did so, she looked back and saw Finn jump for the line. He caught it and began to cross after her, hand over hand.

Coventry flexed her wrist. Her concealed knife dropped into her hand. She held it up and nodded to Finn, thinking it only fair to give him a hint of warning. He started to say something, a protest or denial, but she cut off both words and clothesline with the same quick sweep of her hand. The line parted. Finn swung back the way he had come, slamming into the wall on the other side of the alley. A great many men would have lost their grip in such circumstances and taken a nasty tumble, but he managed to hold on. He dangled there helplessly, better than fifteen feet of air between him and a hard landing.

"Sorry about that, guv," she said, tucking the blade back into its hiding place. Then she took another deep breath and jumped for the roof of the shack, praying it would hold her weight.

Fortunately, it was sturdier than it looked. She nearly lost her footing, but caught herself with one hand and stayed more or less upright. The roof held. She skidded down it just as her cat had done, dropped over the edge, caught the lip with both hands, then let go and fell the last few feet to the ground.

There was Whisper, nonchalantly bathing himself and looking decidedly smug. Coventry shook her head at him. Then she left the alley, walking quickly, not running. A running woman attracted attention. Just before she melted into the crowded street, she took one last look over her shoulder. Finn was climbing doggedly back onto the roof, holding the clothesline and walking up the side of the building.

"Bloody persistent," she repeated.

Chapter 4

Once a few streets separated Coventry from Finn, with no sign of pursuit, she finally had some space in which to think. She slipped into a public house, the best place for ruminations. It was going on noon and the place was full of lads draining their pints and talking loudly. She found a seat near the end of a bench and called for an ale for herself. Whisper had disappeared again. He'd doubtless be lurking somewhere outside.

She considered the choices before her. She had a few pounds tucked in her dress's hidden pocket, but most of her money had been concealed in her red dress and elsewhere in her baggage. Finn would no doubt enjoy a few pints of his own at her expense, she thought angrily. She could live frugally some time on what she had, in addition to purchasing passage to the Continent. But they would look for her on the docks. She would be hunted forever.

She knew that for a certainty. This was no back-alley stabbing. Bartleby Horrocks had been a powerful, important man. The coppers would be searching high and low for his killer. The sad irony was, while they were all chasing Coventry, the man who'd actually done for the blighter could just stroll out of London on the King's highway without a care in the world. It was enough to make one grind one's teeth.

But would they truly watch the docks? Of course they would. While she took pleasure at having temporarily outmaneuvered Finn, he'd found her very quickly. He was smart and he'd learn from the experience. He was young, but that only meant he was vigorous and eager to prove himself. This was a case on which he could build his career. He'd be tenacious and adaptable. And he'd hardly be the only inspector they'd have on the case.

She had to think like the coppers if she hoped to stay a step ahead of them. What would they expect her to do? Flee or go to ground. So they'd be watching the roads and the docks, and meanwhile they'd be searching out her haunts, ferreting out her associates. Would any of the street girls talk? They'd hardly seek out a copper, but if they got dragged in, they'd spill what they had, if only to get out of trouble. And what about Fergie?

Fergie. Coventry's hand clenched on the earthenware mug. If they got to Fergie, they'd find Mr. Horrocks's cufflinks and watch, not to mention his shaving kit and all the rest. That would just be so much more evidence. Well, what of that? It wasn't like they could hang her more than once.

Her best chance was to find a place to hide and wait for the whole business to die down. But that was precisely what the coppers would think she'd do. And this was no nine days' wonder. It wouldn't die down. Not until they had her.

No, that wasn't quite right. The uproar wouldn't subside until they had the murderer. At the moment only two people in London knew Coventry hadn't killed Mr. Horrocks; herself and the real killer. But nobody was looking for the real murderer. They'd be wasting their time on her, and catching her wouldn't do anyone but the true assassin any good.

Somehow, she had to convince Scotland Yard of her innocence. And that meant she had to stop acting guilty. Coventry took a sip of ale. It was foul, nasty stuff, but she'd had worse. What would an innocent girl do? It had been a long time since she'd had to think that way.

She could turn herself in, but she didn't think much of that plan. They'd just believe her to be overcome with remorse, or mad, or more likely they'd simply accept their good fortune and string her up without a second thought.

For a fleeting moment, a truly alarming possibility crossed her mind: *home*. Unbidden, the thought came to her of the house she had once known. Mother. Father. Maybe, if she dared, she could go back. She recalled the story of the Prodigal Son. Would they welcome her with open arms? Would they slaughter the fatted calf and celebrate? For an instant the possibility lay open to her like the pathway to Heaven.

Then the golden moment passed. The pearly gates slammed shut in her face. She was disgraced. Fallen. Unclean. Even if they took her in, out of pure Christian charity, the thought of the shame she would bring to Father's eyes was more than she could bear. And they were such upright, law-abiding folk. Once they learned she was wanted by the police, they would insist on getting to the bottom of the matter. They would make her surrender herself to the coppers. She would break Mother and Father's hearts and it would gain her nothing in the end.

No, she could never, never go home, least of all when she needed help. Coventry blinked away a treacherous tear and drowned the memories with another bitter mouthful of Whitechapel swill.

There was one final option. Unable to run, hide, or surrender, hers was the last chance of the cornered animal: she could fight. Unearth the murderer. Give the coppers their true, proper quarry. The best way for a fox to escape the hounds was to set them on the trail of another fox. Hard luck on that fox, to be sure, but that lad had stuck a knife in Bartleby Horrocks and surely had it coming.

Coventry sat perfectly still, astonished at her own temerity. Her, a fugitive, set herself to catch a desperate killer? It was a mad idea, perfectly mad.

And that, she realized, was why it just might work. Finn Farrell knew she was canny and quick, but she didn't think he thought her mad. This lunatic course might put him out of his reckoning. And even if he did guess her purpose, what of it? That was the one thing that might actually convince him of her innocence. Her relative innocence, admittedly. He knew she was a thief. Whatever had she been thinking, confessing to him like that? But his primary aim was to solve the murder. He might be convinced to overlook her lesser crimes, particularly if she proved of use.

Coventry was a girl not given to heavy introspection. This bout of soul-searching had exhausted her. Then, too, her muscles were weary. But she felt a curious lightness as she stood up from the table. Now she had a plan.

The only difficulty was that she hadn't the slightest idea who else would have wanted to kill Bartleby Horrocks. Besides his presumably long-suffering wife, of course.

"Somewhere to start," Coventry murmured. Clearly, the first thing to do was to discover where Mr. Horrocks had lived. Then she could get inside, have a look around, and see what she could learn of the man. Even if it didn't get her off the hook, she might find out something valuable. Information was currency on the street, more precious than pounds sterling. Knowing something Scotland Yard didn't might buy her a ticket out of this mess.

Madness indeed. Only a lunatic would think of breaking into a dead man's house while sought for his murder. Coventry smiled. She was growing accustomed to the thought and enjoying it more every moment.

Coventry knew she could hardly just traipse into the West End. A few preparations were necessary. One of the first and most important lessons she had learned on the streets was that strangers didn't really see one's face. What they saw were one's clothes. Dress properly for the occasion and no one would question one's right to be there.

The first order of business, therefore, was to get clean. The second was to change clothes. Accordingly, Coventry went to the public bathhouse in Poplar. It took her in the opposite direction from her ultimate goal, but she judged it unlikely anyone would look for her there, so long as she steered clear of the docks. What fugitive would bother with a bath? As she went, she caught occasional glimpses of Whisper out of the corner of her eye. The cat was keeping off the main thoroughfares. It was unusual for him to follow her so closely when she was out and about, but she guessed her extraordinary movements had piqued the feline's curiosity.

Washed and scrubbed clean of dirt, she next went to a dressmaker's, keeping a wary eye out for coppers the while. She explained to the seamstress that she was entering service in Covent Garden and needed a maid's uniform on very short notice. A white apron, crisp and starched, with matching cap, and a black dress of good material would suffice.

"French twill, if you please," she added. It was the best material for early spring. Had the weather been warmer, cotton would have been preferable.

"Three pounds and a shilling," the seamstress said.

"Bit steep, you think?" Coventry retorted, haggling more out of habit than necessity. "Two pounds ten, more like."

"You said you needed it all in a rush," the seamstress said. "Quick or cheap, love. Can't have both."

"And there's me thinking quick and cheap go together," Coventry said. "I'm starting a job here and I've not been paid yet."

"In *some* lines of work they go together, maybe," the seamstress said, arching an eyebrow. "All right, three pounds even, as I'm feeling generous."

"Done."

Coventry left the shop a short while later, wearing her new clothes and carrying her old dress wrapped in paper. She might attract some attention in such attire, but she might not be able to change later. She swiftly hailed a hansom driven by a jovial, red-faced Cockney. His cab was drawn by a fine dark bay Percheron.

"Hello, ma'am," he said. "Where be you a-going?"

She had no idea of the late Mr. Horrocks's address, but could venture a guess. "Covent Garden," she said as she climbed up into the passenger compartment. Whisper, appearing as if by some dark magic, sprang lightly up beside her and sat, tail curled around his paws. She absently stroked his head.

"Right you are," the cabbie said with a broad smile and a friendly wink. It was a tidy distance, about five and a half miles, so he stood to make a good fare. "Hobnobbing with the nobs, are you?"

"Going into service," she said.

"That's good honest work," he said. "My old mum was in service twenty years, till she met my old dad. He was a cabbie what had done all right for himself, so they wed and now here's me, driving the same cab what he drove all them years. It's my legacy, so it is." He affectionately slapped the side of the hansom. "I hope you've the same luck she had."

"And marry a cabbie?" she said, raising a wry eyebrow.

"Why not? Not speaking of myself, I've a wife and three young 'uns at home. But there's plenty of fine lads about."

"I'll keep that in mind," she said diplomatically.

"The address, ma'am? In Covent Garden?"

"Take me to the Market," she said. "I've a few things to pick up on my way."

"Right you are," he said again. "That'll be three shillings thruppence."

He pulled the lever that operated the door as he clicked his tongue and twitched the reins. The horse trotted ahead. Coventry looked out of the cab at the London crowds. She saw a few Bobbies hanging about and resisted the urge to duck or turn away. Better to brazen it out. No fugitive would ride openly about London in a cab, dressed as a domestic servant, so the coppers wouldn't even notice her. At least, that was her hope.

She was either correct or lucky. In either case, the cab traveled quickly and easily across London. Soon the squalid slums of Poplar gave way to the marshy ground near Limehouse, then St. Katherine's Docks and Wapping. The hansom rolled past the Tower of London and on through Blackfriars, finally fetching up at Covent Garden.

It was like traveling to another country, or perhaps another world. The buildings were gracefully constructed and well-kept. The market was every bit as noisy and full of smells and people as the one in Whitechapel, but these people were much better-dressed and cleaner, and the smells more wholesome. Most of the customers were servants.

"Here we are, ma'am," the cabbie called. He opened the trapdoor in the roof of the hansom. Coventry obediently handed up three shillings and three pennies. The cabbie then pulled his lever and opened the main door so she could disembark. It was the normal way of ensuring a passenger did not run and cheat the man of his fare.

She debarked onto the street, Whisper hopping down beside her, and thanked the cabbie, who touched his cap and steered his cab back into the London bustle. Coventry took a moment to get her bearings and picked out a fishmonger.

"Afternoon," Coventry said to the man. She deliberately tempered her Cockney accent to something more moderate, but still the timbre of a working-class girl.

"Afternoon, ma'am," he said. "You have an order?"

"Well, guv, it's like this," she said. "There's a big do at the house this evening, and Cook went and ran short of fish. No one noticed till now. There's an awful row. I thought Cook was like to be sacked. They sent me to see what might be done. Can you make a delivery right away? We're in a right terrible spot."

"I've some fine smelt," the fishmonger said. "How much are you needing?"

"Well," she said, lowering her voice. "It's all a bit confused. See, I'm up at the Horrocks place. You heard the latest?"

The man's eyes widened and his eyes gleamed with gossipy curiosity. "Ah! You don't mean the murder?"

"The very same. So we've all manner of folk coming by. Better too much than too little. Ten pounds ought to do."

"And you don't want to carry it back yourself?"

She shook her head and smiled. "We're dreadful short-handed at present and I may have to go upstairs and wait on the callers. I can't hardly do that smelling of raw fish, can I? Besides, I've one of Madam's dresses here, and it wouldn't do to carry it next to your wares." She gestured to the paper wrapping that actually contained her other dress.

"I see your point. That'll be five crowns."

Coventry managed not to wince. Five crowns would make a significant dent in her finances. Then she realized she needn't pay. "That'll do," she said. "They'll pay you at the house."

"I'll get a lad to run it over directly," the man said. "Hoy! Bill!"

A boy of about fourteen popped up. "What is it, Dad?" he asked.

"Got an order, needs to go straightaway. You know the Horrocks place?"

"Reckon I do, Dad."

"Then get this there, sharpish." The fishmonger had been wrapping fish while he talked. He handed the slightly pungent bundle to the boy, who scampered off.

Coventry followed. This was the tricky part. She had to keep the lad in sight, and London delivery boys were notoriously fleet-footed and hard to pin down. But Coventry was accustomed to moving fast, skirts and stays notwithstanding. She went briskly, giving the boy a bit of a lead but staying within twenty or thirty yards. She'd lost track of Whisper again, but no doubt he knew precisely where she was. She could spare no thought for the cat. He, like herself, would just have to look after himself.

The lad made for Trafalgar Square, hurrying west along Pall Mall. He turned north toward St. James's Square. That was no great surprise. The Square had been the home of dukes, earls, and other fashionable folk for the past two centuries. Many had moved on to Belgravia, further south and west, but some of the more established families still dwelt hereabouts.

The Square was a wide, spacious area of smooth cobblestone with a large fountain pool in the center, ringed by an iron fence. To Coventry, after the close confines of the Whitechapel streets, so much open space was both exhilarating and a little frightening. It reminded her of the countryside, of a well-kept formal garden. She had to swallow a lump in her throat that came at the thought.

The fishmonger's lad made for a large house on the north side of the Square. He went round to the servants' entrance, as expected. Coventry followed at a discreet distance. She kept her head high and her posture straight, making sure to avoid the appearance of skulking. No one looked twice at her; servants were all over the Square, going about their own business. She saw a pair of coppers by the fountain, but they were quite bored and didn't even favor her with a casual once-over. Servants were a common sight on these streets and attracted no notice.

Coventry watched the boy knock at the door. After a moment, the door opened. He held out the fish and held a brief conversation. She wondered what was being said, but could guess. The lad was doing what he'd been told. Whoever had answered the door would either take the fish and pay him, or tell him he'd made a mistake and send him on his way. Either outcome would tell her something about the management of the household.

After a few words had been exchanged, the girl who had answered the door retreated inside. She returned with a stiff-looking fellow who must be the butler. Money changed hands. The girl took the packet of fish. Then the door closed and the boy started back the way he had come. A good lad, Coventry thought, but a bit dull. Obedient enough, but lacking ambition. He could easily have found time for a bit of his own business before returning to his father's market-stall. He'd inherit the family business one day but would rise no higher.

Now she knew how the Horrocks household operated. The servants would assume something untoward was simply a part of the plan they hadn't been told. They might even assume the late Mr. Horrocks had given instructions to which they had not been privy, and he was in no position either to confirm or deny them. That simplified matters considerably. It meant she needn't wait for nightfall and risk housebreaking. She could walk right in, so long as she did it properly.

Supper-time would be best. The butler would be attending the table, along with the footmen. The cook and maids would be busy about the kitchen. She need only worry about a handful of servants, none of whom would be in a position of authority. Coventry was skilled at stealth, but a good bluff often served better than a quiet footstep.

She spent the next couple of hours laying her plans and getting a meal of her own from a cafe. She visited a stationer and requested an embossed sympathy card made out to Mrs. Horrocks, filled with the usual flowery phrases of condolence. She asked that it be signed "Your affectionate friend M." It was a safe guess that Mrs. Horrocks had at least one friend whose name began with that letter. Marys and Margarets were as common as cobblestones.

Then she went to a flower-seller and purchased a fine arrangement of lilies, a flower associated with funerals and death. Coventry's mother had once told her they stood for purity, peace, and compassion, but since becoming acquainted with certain truths of life, Coventry had come to believe they were popular funereal flowers on account of their heavy aroma. Corpses made for foul company, particularly those which had been dead more than a day or two, and strong-smelling flowers were a practical choice.

She made her way back to St. James's Square bearing her floral burden, the card tucked neatly in among the blooms. Under her apron she had tucked her trusty lockpicks and her knife. She might be able to jimmy a pair of handcuffs with hairpins in a pinch, but the well-machined locks in a fine house required better tools.

As she drew near the house, she saw several carriages out-side. Mrs. Horrocks appeared to have a number of distin-guished visitors. So much the better. There would be unfamil-iar faces about the place, possibly including servants from mul-tiple families, which would allay suspicion. She had worried the household might have gone into deep mourning, but apparent-ly the house was receiving visitors, bringing messages of sympa-thy every bit as heartfelt as the one she herself carried.

Coventry took a steadying breath, shifted the flowers in her hand, and walked up to the servant's entrance. She rapped the knocker three times, loudly and firmly.

The pause that followed was encouraging. The longer it took someone to answer the door, the less organized the house-hold was at present. Coventry waited patiently, the scent of lilies filling her nostrils. A familiar black cat poked its head around the corner, blinked at her, and vanished again.

The door swung open to reveal a very young serving-girl, harried and breathless. Several strands of hair trailed from un-der her cap and her face was flushed and sweaty.

"What can I do—" the servant began.

Coventry, half-hidden behind the lilies, simply walked straight forward, trusting the girl to get out of the way. Most people yielded to a decisive movement and this one was no ex-ception. The servant stepped back as she crossed the threshold.

"Got the flowers for Her Ladyship here," Coventry said.

"What flowers?" the girl asked stupidly.

"These bloody flowers," Coventry said impatiently. "The ones for Her Ladyship's room! What blooming flowers did you think I meant? Now, which way? Hurry up, missy, these are bloody heavy!"

"Oh," the girl said sheepishly. "Of course. Down the hall, up the stairs on your left. It's the one at the end of the upstairs hallway."

"Thank you," Coventry said. She kept walking. Behind her, the girl shut the door.

"I'd take you up myself," the girl went on. "Only I've got to get back to the kitchen."

"On your way then," Coventry said. "I can see myself out."

And just like that, with nary a broken window nor jimmied lock, having broken no laws, armed only with flowers and confidence, she had breached the Horrocks house. That, she knew, had been the easy part.

Chapter 5

Coventry climbed the stairs, being careful to keep her face partially screened by the lilies. She heard a hubbub of voices from the direction of the dining room. While she'd never been in this particular house before, she knew the type. Most of them were constructed along similar lines, which made both legitimate work and housebreaking easier. It was odd, she thought, that she would surely be taken for a thief should anyone realize her deception, while she intended no larceny.

That would be just her luck, she thought bitterly. To be taken up by the coppers the one time her intentions were pure. But it wouldn't likely come to that. The card and flowers were her shield. At worst, she'd be told to leave. She'd just have to ensure she wasn't caught red-handed.

Luck was with her. The upstairs hallway was empty, as she had expected. All the servants were seeing to the family and the guests. She walked briskly to the last door, enjoying the feel of rich, thick carpet under her feet and the smell of air that held no stink of coal. She caught the scents of roast meat and fresh-baked bread wafting up the stairs and her mouth watered.

"Mind your business," she murmured under her breath. This was no time to go scrounging food. She shifted the flowers to her left hand, balancing them against her shoulder, and considered the door. It was good, solid wood, carved by an expert. It had a brass-plated lock, but that did not worry her. In all likelihood it would be unlocked, and if not, she had her lockpicks.

She reached for the knob, then hesitated. It was just possible Mrs. Horrocks might have taken to her bed, prostrated with grief—or shamming the same. Best to be safe. She knocked lightly on the door, waited a few breaths, and knocked again. No one answered.

Coventry laid a hand on the knob and slowly turned it. The door swung open silently on well-oiled hinges. She took a quick look back down the hall. It remained empty. She stepped inside and closed the door behind her.

The room was lavishly furnished, hung with several expensive-looking paintings of dour aristocrats. Horrocks ancestors glowered at her from three walls. The fourth held a lovely bay window that overlooked the Square, curtains of rich maroon velvet framing it.

Coventry paused. It really was unusual for Mrs. Horrocks to have so many visitors. The convenience of it for her own endeavors had blinded her to the truth. The widow should be in deep mourning. She should be in seclusion, dressed all in black, receiving no visitors. There ought to be black crepe draped over everything, including the front door and doorknobs. Coventry had seen no such morbid decoration.

A long-buried memory surfaced in her mind. Coventry had once had a little brother, who had taken ill quite suddenly. After a brief illness, he had died. It was a common enough loss, but no less tragic for that, and Coventry remembered her mother weeping. Everywhere she had looked, their house had been swathed in black. She particularly recalled the way every mirror had been covered, as if to see one's own reflection would be somehow indecent.

Now Coventry stared at a large mirror in Mrs. Horrocks's bedroom, the glass scandalously bare. She saw herself, done up in the livery of a domestic servant, holding a bundle of lilies, a silly mooncalf expression on her face. Either Mrs. Horrocks was slow in adopting the trappings of mourning, or she was sufficiently unmoved by her husband's passing to fly in the face of all convention and propriety. Coventry wondered for a moment how the more public parts of the house were adorned. She tucked that thought away and got down to business.

She set the flowers on the nightstand, establishing her alibi for being in the room. Then she examined the area with the cool, professional eye of an experienced thief.

A bloodstained dagger in plain view would be the best evidence, but it seemed Mrs. Horrocks was not quite so close to Lady MacBeth. Still, the widow had a vanity, atop which perched the mirror. Its drawers might contain something of interest.

The left and right drawers held only ordinary combs, cosmetics, and other items of feminine upkeep. But the center drawer was locked, and that was promising. It was the work of a moment to coax the tumblers to yield to Coventry's clever fingers. Inside, she found documents; personal letters, by their look and feel.

Coventry thumbed through them. It appeared Mrs. Horrocks, whose given name was Evelyn, had been carrying on a correspondence with another woman by the name of Caroline, either a close friend or sister. Mrs. Horrocks's own letters, of course, were not to be found, but Coventry thought she might glean something of their contents.

She had no time to peruse the letters in full. She skimmed them, thankful that she, unlike many in her profession, had learned to read at an early age. Words and phrases leapt out at her, words such as "unhappy," "regrettable," "churlish," "beastly," and "scoundrel." These words were directed exclusively at the late Bartleby Horrocks.

"Been complaining about the frying pan, have you, milady?" she mused aloud, lapsing into Cockney slang out of habit and referring to the old man. "Well, that's nothing new. Plenty of cows complain about their mates, but not many stick knives in them. Did you have the grit to do it, love?"

The letters were interesting in a dreary, tawdry sort of way, but they got her no closer to knowing Mrs. Horrocks's inner thoughts. For that, she would need something like a diary.

Coventry nearly slapped her forehead at her own stupidity. Next moment she was at the nightstand, checking the drawers. The top one was locked, but that lock, like the one on the vanity, was a simple little thing she could have sprung with a knife-blade or a pin. Her picks made it child's play. Sure enough, a fine calfskin-bound book lay in the drawer. She opened it, flipped to the end, and began reading the final entry. Mrs. Horrocks's handwriting was graceful and elegant, the pen-strokes looping and swirling in a way that reminded Coventry of fine silver filigree.

March 11

We shall be entertaining tomorrow evening again. More of Bartleby's Parliamentarian acquaintances, including that dreadful Lord Felton and his abominable wife. Frankly, he ought not to bring her to such functions, as her figure could do with a trifle less... trifle. But perhaps that is his design. Feeding such a voracious creature must be expensive, so to farm her out to one's neighbors seems merely prudent. I shall ask Cook to lay in an extra store of pastry against the anticipated culinary emergency.

How tiresome that we must host such folk in the endless process of currying favor. The favors circle round and round, a never-ending cycle of sycophancy. How I do wish we could get out of this dreary city! I have decided, come summer, to abandon London's infernal environs for a more congenial clime and spend a few weeks at the house in Essex.

Bartleby, of course, will remain here, surrounded by his whores and concubines, but at least I shall not suffer the indignity of witnessing it. I cannot help but note that as his waistline advances and his hairline retreats, the cheap hussies on whom he dotes become smaller and younger by the day. I thank God we have no daughters, or... no, perhaps even he would not be so beastly. But his appetite for pretty young things is as insatiable as Lady Felton's belly.

Such is a political marriage. I have heard it said that all politicians are whores, so perhaps Bartleby only seeks his own kind. He certainly shows an ardor with them that I have not felt from him in twenty years or more! And now, with those endless, pointless negotiations with all those tiresome diplomats, he has even more restless energy to expend in sampling such rotten fruits. I wish him joy of them! Should he suffer the obvious consequences of such recklessness, I shall not be one to weep, and if the French pox carries him off, so much the better. It is not as if I were in any danger of contagion!

Ah, but I am being unchristian. It is true, Bartleby is sorely tried by these treaty negotiations and his constant conversations with the Foreign Office. But I do think he might at least consider the appearance of the thing. There is a limit to how many public humiliations a wife may be expected to endure, even one married to a politician.

I close for the night. I find my nerves somewhat frayed. Bartleby will be gone all evening, either working or, more likely, at his hotel room. He thinks I do not know about his lustful boudoir. If all state secrets are so ill-kept, the Empire is surely doomed! I shall take a tincture of laudanum with a cup of tea to help me sleep. May it keep me from bad dreams.

Coventry set the book back in its place and was unsurprised to see a bottle of laudanum next to it. "Damnation," she muttered. It seemed Mrs. Horrocks was not at all enamored of her late husband, but it further appeared she had been at home, drugged and asleep, when Bartleby Horrocks had been killed. It was an odd twist of fate that husband and wife had been under the influence of the same opiate at the same time, in quite separate environs.

She had, however, gleaned some information that might prove useful. Mr. Horrocks had been in the habit of plucking night flowers. That meant some of the other girls might remember him. They might also remember what he liked to talk about. Many men enjoyed talking to tarts. Indulging the lusts of the flesh could be a quite effective method of loosening the male tongue. The diary had given her some idea what sort of girls he liked, which narrowed Coventry's search admirably.

Then there was all that twaddle about diplomats and treaties. Could diplomacy have something to do with the murder? Was it, in fact, a political assassination masquerading as a crime of passion or a robbery?

Regardless, it was high time to be gone. Coventry took a last look around the room. It was obvious this chamber was inhabited only by Mrs. Horrocks. The late Mr. Horrocks doubtless had a bedroom of his own. He also probably had a study, which she would very much like to examine, but that would be risky indeed. Better to get out now, quick and clean. Many a housebreaker had been snared by their own greed.

She opened the bedroom door and stepped out into the upstairs hallway. She retraced her steps toward the stairs. Just down two flights, then out through the servant's door, and she would be in the clear and no one the wiser.

Someone was coming up the stairs. Coventry cursed inwardly, but knew hesitation was her worst enemy. She kept walking like a serving-girl with nothing to hide, keeping her eyes obediently downcast. If one avoided looking in another's face, it was ten to one against being noticed in passing. Two people were coming the opposite direction, a man and a woman.

"I'm sorry for the inconvenience," the man was saying as they passed her. His voice was unmistakably Irish—and distinctly familiar.

A jolt of pure terror shot down Coventry's spine. Her blood went suddenly icy. It wasn't possible! There was no chance, none! She willed herself not to flinch, to just keep walking. It was far too late to do anything but brazen it out. Everything was all right. He hadn't been looking for her, hadn't thought to look closely at the face of just another serving girl. Men saw the uniform, not the woman beneath it. Her distinctive auburn hair was hidden under her cap. She was in a different place, a different costume. He hadn't noticed her.

"Half a moment, please," Finn Farrell said. "Miss? Pardon me."

Coventry pretended not to hear. Every step she took was one step closer to freedom.

A hand, strong and heavy, came down on her shoulder.

"Now just where—" Finn began.

Coventry didn't try to shake free. He'd be expecting that. Instead, she grabbed his wrist with both hands and pulled as hard as she could, twisting her body sharply to the side as she did.

This would not have worked on level ground, but they were on a staircase. Finn was two steps higher than Coventry and his weight was already shifted downward. The sudden increase in momentum hurled him past her toward the landing. He let go of her shoulder with a startled cry. She released his wrist and watched him tumble, his body banging and bouncing on the steps. They were carpeted, but the carpet was thin and beneath it was hard wood.

Coventry had a split second to make up her mind whether to continue down or to run back upstairs. Finn twisted like a snake, snatching at the bannister with his left hand. By some combination of keen reflexes and sheer luck, he caught the railing as he fell backward, arresting his descent. He stared up at her, eyes wide with shock and surprise, scrambling to get his feet back under himself.

She dared not risk a dash past him. She spun and sprinted up the stairs. A maid stood just above her, hands raised in horror, a scream just beginning to emerge from her wide mouth. Coventry, in no mood to be polite, seized the maid's apron-strings and yanked her downward, using the force of the motion to pull herself faster. The maid bounced down several steps with a shriek that turned to an almost soundless whoosh of breath when she struck one of the stairs.

Finn hurdled the tumbling body of the maid and gave chase. Coventry could hardly believe the man's speed. She'd bought only a few seconds' lead, with no plan and nowhere to go. She was on the back stairs. There was certainly a front staircase, too. If she could get there, and slow the copper somehow, she just might make it to the street. There was little point thinking farther ahead than that. She'd think of something when she got there.

The hallway was regrettably empty of large vases or suits of armor that might be cast into Finn's path. Coventry simply ran, cursing the long skirt that tried to tangle her feet. The main stair was just ahead. She put her head down and sprinted for all she was worth.

Finn flung himself into a headlong lunge, catching the tip of her shoe with one hand. Coventry stumbled and went down, sliding past the head of the stairs. Hot, fierce pain ripped along the flesh of her arm as she skidded across the carpet. She rolled, got a hand under herself, and came up on one knee.

Finn was already rising to his feet. He had lost a button from his waistcoat and his tie was badly askew, but he had no new injuries. He was strong, solid, and now standing between her and the stairs.

"Bloody hell," she spat between gasps for breath. "What's the matter with you, you bastard? You're always in my bloody way!"

"Here now," Finn said in tones more reasonable than the situation really warranted. "There's no call for that, lass. If you'll recall, I've done you no harm. It's you who's insisting on fighting. I'll be needing you to come with me, of course."

"Bugger that and bugger you," she snarled. She reached under her apron and drew her knife. She flexed her wrist and made sure he could see the blade. "I'll give you an anointing you'll not forget, you hugger-mugger gibface baboon! You think I did you the first time, with that pretty shiner you're sporting? I'll batty-fang you proper, you touch me again!"

Finn's eyebrows went up. "There's some lads would take offense to those words, lass. Assuming they could understand them."

She waved the knife threateningly. "Back off!" she warned, getting the rest of the way to her feet and advancing a pace. "You think I won't do it? You're so sure I'm a bloody murderer already!"

He reached into his coat and drew out his wooden truncheon. He held it in one hand with a worrying nonchalance that suggested he knew very well how to use it. He didn't get out of the way. Instead, he shifted his balance slightly to the balls of his feet, tensing for battle.

"That's one of the things we're needing to talk about," he said. "That, and the pair of handcuffs you borrowed."

"And here's me thinking they were a gift," Coventry said, starting to sidle along the wall toward the stairs. "Nice pair of bracelets for a pretty girl."

"I don't suppose you still have them?" he inquired politely, sidestepping to block her path.

"Got rid of them," she said. "They didn't match my hair."

"It's a fine shade," he agreed. "The way the red blends with the brown, it's got a right lovely sheen to it. And you're right, bronze or copper might be a better color on you, but a lad's got to go with what's available. Here's your problem, lass. You're carrying that knife, but you're not prepared to use it."

"Come one step closer and you'll see how ready I am," she retorted, retreating and circling to the other side of the hallway. She could hear a gathering uproar downstairs. The maid had roused the household. There'd be men in plenty coming up those stairs in a matter of moments.

"If you'd wanted to stab me, you'd have done it when you slipped your bracelets back in Whitechapel," he said, sliding his feet across the carpet, keeping his balance, staying in front of her. "It was careless of me not to check you for weapons. You've a rather disarming manner about you, which kept me from disarming you."

"That was before I knew how bloody-minded stubborn you were," she said. "And if I put you off your guard, that's more fool you."

"Fair enough," he agreed. "I deserved it when you gave me the slip. I'm not angry." Then he lunged.

Coventry tried to step back, but Finn was as quick as she and his arms were longer. His truncheon clipped her forearm, knocking her knife-hand to one side. Then he was inside her reach, grabbing her right wrist in his left hand. Coventry saw his right arm poised, the stout piece of wood hanging over her head, but she was frantic to escape, beyond all thought of surrender. She sank her teeth into his left hand just behind the thumb, biting down with all her strength.

The blow from the truncheon was like a thunderclap. Bright stars flashed in front of Coventry's eyes. Her legs went wobbly and collapsed under her. She tasted blood on her tongue and wondered dizzily if it was hers or Finn's. Dimly, as if from a great distance, she heard a muffled clink as her knife fell to the floor. She followed it down. Darkness rushed into her vision on all sides, leaving the world as a blurred, distant circle of light, like the end of a railroad tunnel.

"Here, lass," someone was saying in surprisingly gentle tones. "Just lie down. I'm sorry, darling. Didn't mean to hit you so hard. Bloody hell, what a dog's breakfast this turned out to be."

Coventry just lay there. Moving did not seem nearly so important as it had a moment before. She felt very little pain, only a great heaviness in all her limbs and a thickness in her head, as if her brain was swaddled in layers of thick velvet. She tried to speak, but her tongue felt swollen and numb.

"Don't just stand there gaping, miss," the voice said. It was speaking to someone else now, a note of sharp command in it. "There's a pair of coppers out on the Square. Run and tell them Detective Farrell needs them. Then fetch a doctor. Quick, lass."

Coventry heard a hubbub of voices, male and female. It reminded her of waves crashing against the rocks on the seashore. She thought of holidays by the sea when she had been young, the feel of the water around her ankles, the taste of salt on her lips.

"A damp cloth, if you please," the voice said, talking to yet another person. "Move!"

Coventry drifted. For some time she was conscious only of that strange lassitude. Her arms seemed burdened by tremendous weights. She saw only darkness and strange, remarkable splashes of color.

Something cool and wet was laid against her brow. It felt nice; pleasant. The voice was talking to her, speaking kindly, soothing words, gentle words she'd not heard in a very long time. A hand was holding hers. She squeezed it, taking comfort from the contact.

More hands laid hold of her, shifting her, picking her up and laying her on something flat and rather hard. Coventry made a weak sound of distress.

"Easy now, lads," the voice said. "Don't jostle her."

"We taking her to Newgate, guv?" a new voice said.

"None of that," the first voice said.

"The Yard, then?"

"Nay, best take her to Chelsea."

"Chelsea, guv?"

"Aye, lad. Chelsea Hospital for Women. You know where that is, don't you?"

"Well, yes, guv, but... I mean, she's the one what stabbed the Minister, right? She's a prisoner, isn't she?"

"Of course she's a prisoner! But she's hurt! So she's going to the bloody hospital!"

Someone guffawed. "Can't be cheating old Jack Ketch out of his day's work, can you? Don't want to get on the hangman's bad side!"

"I've cracked one head today," the first voice said coldly. "Care to make it two?"

There was a short pause. Then, in sullen but respectful tones, the other man said, "Right you are, guv."

Strong hands picked Coventry up. She was lifted and borne out of the house, into the bright sunlight. She closed her eyes but the rays pierced her lids and her brain. Her world went white and blank.

Chapter 6

There was pain; a heavy, monotonous throbbing in her skull. When she dared open her eyes, light stabbed into her brain and she quickly closed them again. That glimpse had shown her lamplight, not very bright in truth. But her whole head felt tender and sensitive, particularly her left temple. The skin there was stretched tight, radiating heat and pain from a swelling that seemed enormous.

She raised a hand to probe at the injury, to see if it really was as large as it felt from within. Her arm moved only a few inches. Then something prevented further motion. She became conscious of something wrapped around her wrist, restraining her.

"You're awake," a male voice said. "That's grand. I've been worrying."

The voice was familiar. She knew it from somewhere. She licked her lips and tried to form words with a thick and clumsy tongue.

"Father?" she croaked.

"What's your father's name, lass? I can send word to him, if you'd like."

But awareness was coming back to Coventry now, and with it came wariness and memory, unreliable though she knew it to be. "Finn Farrell," she said in a flat voice.

"Aye, that's myself," he said agreeably.

"Nice try," she said. "I'll not talk so easily."

"Can't blame a lad for trying. Can you open your eyes, lass?"

She tried it again, more carefully this time. She saw an oil lamp a few feet away. In its light she saw Finn's face, bending toward hers. Her first impression, curiously, was of kindness in his eyes. Then she took in the rest of his appearance. His cheek was crusted with dried blood and the flesh around one eye was dark and puffy. He held the lamp in a hand that was swathed in a white bandage.

"Water," she whispered.

"Of course," he said. He set the lamp on a nearby table and picked up an earthenware mug. "Easy, now."

He gingerly slipped a hand behind her neck, helping her elevate her head. With his other hand, the bandaged one, he held the cup to her lips. She swallowed several mouthfuls of water, cleaner than any that could be found in Whitechapel or Poplar. In the East End one drank ale when possible, for the water was downright dangerous.

"Better, lass?" he said.

She nodded. "You look one of the puppets in a Punch and Judy," she said. "Been picking fights in pubs?"

He smiled. "Ran afoul of a wild alley-cat," he said. "She'd a fine pair of claws on her and a right vicious bite."

"If you're waiting for an apology, you'll be here all night," she said. "And you still won't get one."

"I'm wanting to know what you were doing in the Horrocks house," he said.

"I could ask you the same."

His mustache twitched with what might have been a suppressed laugh. "I'm doing my duty, madam. I'm investigating a murder."

"Which I didn't commit," she said.

Finn tapped his chin with his forefinger. "This murder you didn't commit. Would this be the same murder that was done in a hotel room you were seen entering, dressed as a common tart, with the victim, and leaving later, alone? The victim whose house you were taken in, dressed as a servant, not twenty-four hours later?"

"I wasn't dressed so common as all that," Coventry said sullenly. "My best bloody dress, that was. The one you've stolen off me."

"It's been taken up as evidence," he gently corrected her. "Not stolen."

"The government's got it and I don't. Call it what you like, I call it bloody theft. And you'll find no blood on it because I didn't bloody well stab him!"

"So you insist," he said. "What were you doing in the Horrocks house?"

"I wasn't stealing," she said.

"No," he said thoughtfully. "I don't suppose you were."

She blinked in surprise. "You believe me?"

He nodded. "Aside from that nasty little piece of cutlery you were carrying, all we found on your person was a set of lockpicks that'd be the envy of the hardest Newgate box-man and a few quid in loose coin and banknotes. You hadn't a thing of value you'd have found in the house. And you were on your way out, not in, when I saw you. If you're a burglar, you're quite a poor one. So I ask you again, what were you doing?"

She set her jaw. "You wouldn't believe me if I told you."

"I believed the last thing you said," he said. "Doesn't that win me any credit?"

"You broke my bloody head with that damned hickory stick of yours!"

"You were gnawing my hand at the time," he said, but for the first time in the conversation, his gaze wavered. "But I am sorry for striking you so hard. Perhaps I should tell you, before they made me a detective, I worked the docks. I'm accustomed to brawling with drunken longshoremen. Those lads know how to take a hit, and give one, too. When I felt your teeth in my flesh, I fell back on old habits. I'd meant only to give you a light tap, knock some of the fight out of you, but you don't fight like a wee lass. You scrap better than many a lad I've tangled with, and I'm from Ireland!"

Coventry tried again to touch her head and tugged on her restraints. She looked down and saw she was secured to the bed by leather straps on both wrists, fastened with heavy iron buck-les. She was still clad in her maid's dress, but the apron had been removed. She sagged back and glared at Finn, fighting a rising feeling of panic, hiding it behind her anger.

"Does it excite you, a strong blighter like yourself, tying a girl down? Seeing her squirm? Does it put life in your bloody pecker, berk?"

"I've not forgotten the way you slipped my bracelets," he said, unperturbed. "So I'm taking no chances. You're a sight more dangerous than you look, Miss Adams. But we've wandered off the subject. For the third time, what were you doing in that house?"

"I was looking for clues," she said.

It was his turn to look startled. "Really? Clues pertaining to what, exactly?"

"To the murder, of course! Same as yourself! I thought maybe I could find out who killed the bastard!"

He leaned in closer. "Who are you working for?" he asked quietly.

"What?" She didn't understand. Her heart was racing, her breathing speeding up. Memories were swimming to the surface of her mind, memories of being bound and helpless. She needed to get out of the restraints, to be free.

"The French?" he guessed. "Or the Russians, maybe? The Turks?"

"What the bloody hell are you babbling about?"

"I'm thinking you were looking for Horrocks's correspondence," he said. "About the treaty. Ahead of Parliament's vote tomorrow."

"Why would I care a fig what those toffs are nattering about? I didn't know about the bloody Foreign Office till I saw his wife's diary!"

"Why would you care about Mrs. Horrocks's diary?" Finn asked. "She's got nothing to do with Parliament."

"I thought maybe she'd killed him," Coventry said. "Out of jealousy."

It was Finn's turn to look very confused. "Either this was an assassination or he was done in by a lady of the night," he said. "If the latter, you're likely the killer. If the former, you're still the most likely suspect. Except..."

"Except I've never killed a man in my life!" she snapped.

"Then why do you carry that knife?"

"Protection."

"Protection you're unwilling to use?"

"I never said I wouldn't use it. I said I'd never killed!" She snorted, which made her head throb all the worse. Indignation was helping her forget her situation, which was some comfort, though fear was still bubbling in her like a slow-boiling cauldron. "There's a vast bloody distance between leaving a lad in the pink of health and killing him. You say you walked the dockyard beat, once on a time. When?"

"Just last year. I've not been a detective long."

"Ever heard of a bloke called Handsome Hal?"

Finn nodded. "Aye, Hal Holcomb. A right nasty piece of work by all accounts. A whoremaster, makes his living trading in young lasses' flesh. What's he got to do with this?"

"You know how he got his nickname?"

He tapped his chin with his forefinger again, recalling. "Scars," he said. "Quite the remarkable set of scars he's carrying, if memory serves."

"Who do you think gave him those marks?"

Finn actually laughed aloud. Then he saw the look in her eye and stopped laughing. "You've a fine set of claws, darling, as I said."

"If I was ever to kill anyone," she said grimly, "it would've been him."

"He mistreated you?" Finn guessed. "You were one of his girls?"

"He thought so," she said bitterly. "I don't work for any man."

"No, I imagine you wouldn't," he said softly. "But someone hired you to break into the Horrocks house."

"I never did! I knocked on the door and they let me in! I broke nothing!"

"Why would they let you in?"

She smiled. "I was dressed as a maid and carrying a bundle of lilies."

He laughed again. "Excellent! You've a fine head on your shoulders, and I apologize again for damaging it. No, you're quite right, madam. They'd hardly stop to question you. Who *are* you?"

"What do you mean?"

"I've known a great many girls of the street," he said.

"That's hardly something to boast of," she retorted.

"I'm not speaking biblically," he said. "I mean to see and speak with. You're the cleverest of the bunch by a fair sight. You're an educated lass. Your Cockney accent's good, don't mistake me, but it's like that maid's outfit you're wearing, or the tart's dress you had on last night. It's naught but a costume. When you called me 'Father' when you woke, you didn't use it. You sounded right posh, if you'll pardon me. And if your right name's Coventry Adams, I'll take out my badge of office and eat it, one bite at a time, right here in front of you."

"The paper was right about you," Coventry said.

"What paper?"

"The *Times*. It said you're a rising star."

"I don't read the papers. I prefer to get my news straight off the streets."

"You're a smart lad for doing it," she said. "So be smart now. Think! I'm trying to get you off my bloody back, aren't I? You were already looking for me. I'm no bloody spy! I thought I could get clear of you if I could prove who really killed Horrocks. That's who you should be looking for."

"And I suppose you've some ideas?" he asked.

"Nothing I could swear to," she admitted. "It would have to be someone who knew where he'd be. They had to know his habits, know he'd be at the hotel instead of at home last night. His wife's diary said he liked to pick up girls like me."

"So he'd a routine," Finn said. "Someone might have followed him, or lain in wait."

"When did they find the body?" she asked.

"A little past midnight," he said. "One of the other patrons reported hearing sounds of a struggle."

"That's not possible," Coventry said.

"I assure you, it's what he said," Finn said. "I spoke to the Bobby who took the report."

She shook her head. "No, I mean, there couldn't have been a struggle."

"Why not?"

"Because he was flat on his back from bloody laudanum! You could've set off a cannon in his room and he'd not have stirred!"

"You drugged him," Finn said.

"I didn't say that," she said.

He smiled wryly. "Nay, you didn't. But if he was unconscious when he was stabbed..."

"No one would have heard a thing," Coventry said. "No screams, no struggle. Your witness is lying."

"Someone definitely is," Finn said.

"You think it's me?" she asked indignantly.

"For a lass who won't tell me her true name, who hides everything about herself and who enjoys wearing disguises, you're showing a bit of cheek asking to be taken at face value."

"Fair enough," Coventry admitted. "But I'm not lying about this!"

"Laudanum," Finn said absently. "If Horrocks was stabbed in a stupor, there'd have been no screaming, no fighting, no struggle. And no one else at the hotel heard a thing. Just the one patron. So that must mean…"

They looked at one another. "He's the killer," they said in unison.

There was a brief pause. Then Finn sprang to his feet.

"Where the hell are you going?" Coventry demanded.

"To the hotel," he said.

"And you're leaving me here?" she said, shaking her wrists. "Like this?" Panic leapt up in her again.

"You'll be safe until I get back," he said. "You're at Chelsea Hospital, in a private room, with a Bobby outside your door. Don't fret, nobody will harm you, nor even touch you. I apologize for the discourtesy, but I can't have you running off again. I'll be needing you as a witness at the very least, and I've a notion you'll disappear if given half the chance. We'll talk further when I return."

He touched his hat in a brief, polite gesture, then dashed out of the room.

"Finbar Farrell!" Coventry shouted. "Get back here! I'm not done with you!"

But the door slammed shut and he was gone. A key turned in the lock.

Coventry's inner voice was screaming. She was trapped, tied to a bed, helpless, at the pleasure of men who would use her and hurt her. The panic boiled over and she began to thrash, fighting her restraints foolishly, wasting her strength. She was so far gone that she had no idea whether her screams were real or only in her head.

Finally, after a few minutes or hours, she returned to herself. Her heart still pounded, but it returned to something like a steady rhythm. She ceased her rapid, panicked breaths and let her lungs fill themselves all the way. Her wits remained scrambled, but she held an internal debate, such as she could.

Finn's not so bad as all that.

Pull the other one, love, it's got bells on it! He cracked your bloody skull!

But he feels bad about it. Besides, I did draw a knife on him. He could've hauled me to Newgate Prison, chucked me in with the cutpurses and murderers. I could be on my way to Tyburn Cross this very moment, but he took me to hospital instead. He's all right, I tell you.

So he's all right. Maybe. What bloody difference does that make? Remember what happened last time you trusted a man?

I'm helping him. He'll remember it.

Don't ever depend on gratitude. Gratitude isn't worth shite on the street. The only thing most blokes care about is what you can do for them here and now. If he keeps you around, it's because he wants something.

I could make him want me. I'm good at that. And he's not a bad-looking bloke, come to that. It might be worth it to have a protector. He's got gentle hands.

When he's not breaking heads with them! Men have only ever wanted one thing from you, and they're not bloody gentle about it once you're on your back! You have to get out, love. Run and keep running! Don't ever depend on anyone, least of all a man. If he's bad, he'll hurt you. If he's decent, he'll let you down.

I did help him. And he'll remember, I tell you!

Oh, that's nice. That's bloody brilliant. Keep dreaming, love. But your problem remains.

He's gone looking for the murderer. I can't help him chase that bloke down, not with what little I know. Don't even know what he looks like. But I can find something else. If this was done by one of those toffs in Parliament, the bastard didn't likely get his own hands dirty. But maybe he'll have a record of the lad who did.

You're mad! You can't go poking around Parliament! You know who sits in the House of bloody Lords! Your bloody father, that's who! And he's not the only one who'd know you on sight!

Coventry scowled at herself. That was a nasty, mean-spirited thrust. But it was a valid concern. She had known several MPs back in the old days. They might not recognize her if they saw her, but it was a risk. Then there was her family to consider. Anyway, all that was beside the current point, which was that she was shackled to an iron bedframe.

"First things first," she muttered aloud, fighting a fresh wave of panic. She craned her neck toward the door. It was closed, and looked sturdy, but a loud noise might carry to the copper standing guard. She'd have to be quiet about this.

She examined her bindings, tugging first sharply, then more steadily, testing their strength. The leather was fairly new and supple. It wouldn't give easily. She couldn't break them by force. Nor could she reach the buckles with either hand.

Coventry tightened the muscles in her belly and sat up. She tried to curl her head down to her wrists. She couldn't quite reach with her teeth. The restraints were secured to the bedframe about halfway along its length, between two of the slats. She couldn't slide them far in either direction.

But she could move herself. "Should've tied my ankles while you were at it," she whispered with grim satisfaction. "You're too much of a bloody gentleman by half, Finn Farrell." Using the leather bindings to brace herself, she thrust her legs off the end of the bed and pulled herself downward.

She fell onto her back as her feet shot out into the air. She kept her hips balanced precariously on the very bottom of her mattress. Her feet dangled some distance from the floor. And her hands were now at the level of her face.

The leather tasted oily but not too unpleasant. The buckles were fastened tightly, so she had to work and worry at the strap to get a little slack, but once she managed to sink her teeth in, she was able to pull her right-hand strap loose. After that, it was the work of a moment to free her left hand as well.

She sat up again and considered her next move. As she did so, she absentmindedly unfastened one of the straps from the bed. It might prove of some use. She had few enough tools available to her. A quick examination of her dress revealed, to no great surprise, that her lockpicks and knife had been taken. Her shoes, also, were not in the room. Coventry grimaced at the thought of prancing over the hard, dirty London cobbles in her stocking feet. But she'd done worse things while wearing less.

She immediately discarded any idea of going out by the door. The copper might be susceptible to persuasion, but just as likely he'd be a stolid, dull sort, determined to do his duty. She had no illusions about her chances of overpowering him and she daren't try her charms. That left the window. She went to it and found there were no bars on the glass, which was good, but her room was two stories above ground, which was not. The window overlooked a side street, on which she could see some evening traffic coming and going, but a fog was rising, as it often did this time of night. So much the better, if she could once get down.

Coventry tried the window latch. The metal was damp and rusted and would not budge. She might be able to shift it by main force, but not without making a terrible racket. Breaking the window would actually be quieter.

She went back to her bed and quickly stripped off the linens. The table seemed a light and flimsy thing to which to entrust her safety, but it would have to suffice. She lacked the strength to move the heavy iron bed so far, and wouldn't have been able to do it quietly. She swiftly knotted one end of the bedsheet to the table leg and placed it at the windowsill. It would only give her a few feet of extra height, but every inch would be a help.

The other thing she must do was slow any pursuit. Coventry wrestled the mattress off the bed and slid it to the door, propping it against the wood. It would at least inconvenience anyone trying to come in, particularly if they did not expect it. As an afterthought, she balanced the lamp carefully atop the mattress's edge. Now, if it was pushed aside, the lamp would fall and shatter. It was unlikely to cause a serious fire, for the floor was hardwood and would not blaze up easily, but it would certainly create distraction and possible panic. That was good; she had no wish to burn down the hospital.

Her preparations nearly complete, Coventry wrapped the leather strap around her right hand, taking care to cover her knuckles. Then, with her makeshift glove, she punched through the windowpane.

The glass shattered into a thousand tinkling shards. Most of them spun into the night, falling like flakes of ice to the street below, but several jagged pieces remained in the frame. Still using the leather strap to protect her hand, she cleared the dangerous bits away.

"Here now! What's all that in there?" the copper called through the door in the typical blustering fashion of a London Bobby.

Coventry, already halfway out the window, did not bother to answer. She took a firm grip on the bedsheet and let herself drop.

The fall was short, but terrifying. The sheet pulled suddenly taut, snapping her against the brick wall. Her hands slipped. She clutched with the strength of panic and held onto the very end of the sheet. There she dangled, looking down at some ten feet of open air between her and the hard cobbles.

Over her head, she heard the crash of breaking glass, the muffled roar of flames as the spilt lamp-oil caught, and a shout of alarm. "Fire!" the copper exclaimed, a cry sure to raise the whole neighborhood.

Coventry sucked in a breath and let go of the sheet.

She tried to bend her knees when she landed, to take some of the shock, but the hard stones sent a jarring pain all the way up past her knees. The cobbles were damp with the evening fog and one foot slipped out from under her. She fell onto her side and her head struck the cobbles. A bolt of terrible pain went straight through her skull, blinding her with its sheer intensity. It was like being struck by lightning.

She lay for a moment, stunned. She was dimly aware of a horse that appeared suddenly from the fog, drawing a two-wheeled hansom. Acting on dumb instinct, her thoughts still dazed, she rolled to one side. Horses, fortunately, liked to tread on humans only marginally better than humans liked to be trodden on, and this animal was no exception. It shied to one side, snorting, and paused.

"Go on, lad!" the driver snapped, flicking his whip. In the darkness and fog, he had not seen Coventry in her black dress as she lay in the street.

On impulse, she scrambled up behind the coach and took hold of the bars that supported the rear of the conveyance. She hung on with what was left of her strength, managing to raise her feet above the axle.

The coachman, sitting scant inches above her, had not noticed his uninvited passenger. He sent the whip whistling above the horse's ears again and they trotted on into the gathering London night.

Chapter 7

Coventry dropped off the back of the hansom a couple of streets later. Full night had fallen, for which she was glad. Between the darkness, the fog, and her black dress, she was nearly invisible so long as she kept out of the halos cast by the gaslights. Her stockinged feet found the slick cobbles treacherous. Wet coldness soaked up into her from below, sapping her strength. She had regained her freedom, but she needed shelter, food, and warmth.

She picked out the nearest likely-looking house, making sure to choose a large, prosperous dwelling. She went to the servants' entrance, taking a moment to dishevel herself a bit further, taking off her maid's cap and stowing it away, then drawing her hair down her face so she looked particularly bedraggled. As an afterthought, she found a protruding bit of rough iron on a nearby fence-rail and scored her fingertip, drawing a bright bead of blood. She smeared a bit of the blood on her cheeks. Then she thought sad, dreadful thoughts for a few moments.

Coventry's life had been difficult these past years, but she had largely lost the impulse to shed tears. Those first days, when Handsome Hal had taken her under his "protection," she had sobbed so hard she had thought her throat might tear itself out of her body, but now she had few tears left. She was forced to go back to childhood memories, to think not of pain but of long-lost kindnesses. She thought of the pony she had ridden as a young girl; the dark, liquid eyes, the velvety nose she so loved to kiss, the way the horse's lips tickled her palm when she held out a lump of sugar. She thought of Mother and the warm, welcoming arms which had shielded her from a world whose cruelty she had not yet imagined.

Coventry swallowed and felt her eyes filling. It would suffice. She walked to the door, making herself stumble slightly as she went, and knocked quietly, hesitantly.

After a long moment, the door opened. In Whitechapel, the appearance of an apparition such as herself on the doorstep would invite suspicion and the door would be slammed in her face, or more likely never opened in the first place. But this was Chelsea, a fine neighborhood, a safe place, and the young servant-girl who stood in the doorway was shocked, but not frightened.

"Oh, miss!" the girl cried, putting a hand to her mouth. "Whatever is the matter?"

"Please," Coventry whispered, holding out a trembling hand. A tear began to trickle down her cheek. "Help me."

"Oh, you poor thing!" the girl said. "Do come in! I'll just fetch Mrs. Lennox! Half a moment!"

Coventry let the girl lead her into the kitchen, where she was ushered onto a wooden stool before the fire. It was almost too easy to act the part of a shaking, pathetic wretch. The cook and another servant looked at her curiously.

"What's this, Mary?" the cook asked the girl who had brought her in, but Mary was already rushing to find the housekeeper.

In the absence of anyone else to interrogate, the cook and her underling began peppering Coventry with questions. In response, she simply buried her head in her hands and convincingly sobbed. Getting no answers, the servants soon returned to their work, though they cast frequent looks in her direction.

Soon enough, Mary returned in the company of a brisk, no-nonsense woman of middle years. Tall, thin, and stern, Mrs. Lennox appeared formidable and, to judge by the deferential attitudes of the other servants, she commanded considerable respect.

"What are you thinking, Mary?" Mrs. Lennox demanded in a broad Yorkshire accent. "You just cast the poor thing loose here in the kitchen?"

"She looked cold, Mrs. Lennox," Mary said, her eyes downcast. "I thought the fire might do her some good."

"The poor girl is humiliated!" Mrs. Lennox snapped. "And you leave her here for anyone in the household to gawk at? What are you all staring at?" she added, turning her eye on the others, who immediately became very busy about the kitchen putting away the supper dishes.

Mrs. Lennox put a hand on Coventry's shoulder. Coventry made herself flinch away from the contact and whimpered like a beaten puppy.

"You just come with me," Mrs. Lennox said. "Come along, lass."

Slowly, reluctantly, Coventry got to her feet and followed the housekeeper, who led her up the back stair to a small room that was, she realized, where Mrs. Lennox herself slept. The door was shut behind them. She jumped at the sound, as if she were startled by loud noises.

"Now then," Mrs. Lennox said, and Coventry was genuinely surprised by the change in her. The stern taskmistress vanished, and in its place was a motherly woman with soft eyes and gentle hands. "What's your name, my dear, and what household do you belong to?"

"E-Esther, ma'am," Coventry stammered. "I'm... I'm a new girl at the Meltons," she added, recalling a family which had lived in Chelsea the last she'd heard and silently praying this was not their house.

"There now, Esther, it's all right," Mrs. Lennox said. "Do you know where you are?"

Coventry shook her head. "No, ma'am. I... I was on my way home and I took a shortcut across the Gardens. I... some men... they found me there..."

"Oh, lass," Mrs. Lennox said, her own eyes growing moist. "Don't you know better than to wander such places after dark by yourself?"

"I was late coming home," Coventry said, looking down at the floor. "I was in a hurry. I didn't want to be late. Please, Mrs. Lennox, don't... don't tell them at the house. I'll lose my position, so I will, and they'll have me out on the street."

Mrs. Lennox clucked her tongue. "Nonsense. No one need know about your misfortune. I understand, lass." She laid a hand on Coventry's arm. "No one but a woman knows the secret shame we must sometimes bear. They'll hear nothing from me, and I'll see the others don't talk. You're at the Conway House, and I'd never have it said we didn't have charity on those less fortunate. You look to be about the same size as Mary. I'll fetch you a spare dress of hers and we'll make a swap. Yours is a little the worse for wear, but nothing I can't mend. I think we've an old pair of shoes somewhere about that just might do, and we'll get you a cap."

"Oh, thank you, ma'am," Coventry said, her voice breaking slightly. "You're ever so kind." She felt bad to be playing a trick on this kindhearted woman, but she reminded herself that her need was genuine. Perhaps she might find the chance to repay such generosity.

"Nonsense," Mrs. Lennox said again. "Young lasses in service need a mother every now and again, that's all. Are you hungry, dear?"

"Yes, a bit," Coventry said. Her stomach was hollow and empty. The thought of food set her mouth to watering.

"We've some leftovers from supper," Mrs. Lennox said, all brisk business again. "You just stay here, lass. I'll be back directly. There's water in the basin. You'll want to clean up your face and perhaps do something with your hair."

Coventry couldn't help a quick glance around Mrs. Lennox's room while the other woman was away, out of habit, but she firmly resisted looking for precious things or money. She'd rob those who could afford it, the fat men who took advantage of girls like herself, with nary a regret, but she'd never steal from a Good Samaritan.

When Mrs. Lennox came back, she had a clean, dry maid's dress over her arm, a pair of shoes in one hand, and a plate in the other. On the plate were a bread roll, some bits of cold roast beef, and a piece of Yorkshire pudding.

"Now," Mrs. Lennox said. "Try these on and we'll get this food in you."

The clothing was an excellent fit. Once she was dressed, Coventry gave Mrs. Lennox a shy smile. The food was delicious. She really did feel better once she had eaten.

"I'd best be getting back to the house now, ma'am," she said. "They'll be missing me. I'll be in trouble enough as it stands."

Mrs. Lennox nodded. "Of course, lass. And don't worry yourself. You think you're the only girl this has happened to? Shame is only shame if the world knows. You'll be all right."

Coventry felt a sudden burning behind her eyes which was unfeigned. "If only, ma'am," she whispered. "Thank you kindly for the clothes and the food. And you won't... tell anyone, will you?"

"Who would I tell?" The older woman seemed startled, almost offended.

"The police?"

"What business is it of theirs? It's not like they'd do anything. They'd only make you a public spectacle."

Coventry nodded. She tucked her hair under the new cap, set her jaw, and gave what she hoped looked like a brave attempt at a smile.

"Off you go, then," Mrs. Lennox said. "Do you need someone to walk you home? I can get one of the lads."

Coventry shook her head. "No thank you, ma'am. I'd rather they not think I was stepping out with a boy, if you know what I mean."

"Of course. But you be careful, lass. Now and in future."

Coventry stepped out of the house into the fog's chilly embrace. She still had no money, nothing but the clothes on her back, but her luck had turned. She could feel it. All she needed now was a place to sleep. Come morning, she had a plan.

A drowsy gentleman stumbling out of his club just down the street provided a pocketbook which proved to contain fifty pounds in banknotes. Thus equipped, Coventry rented a room at the Grosvenor Hotel on Buckingham Palace Road. She did not do so under her own name, of course, nor even pretend to act on her own behalf. She claimed to be needing accommodation for Lady Winthrop. There was no Lady Winthrop, at least not so far as Coventry knew, but she said the name with such respect that the hotel manager dared not admit his ignorance.

"Her Ladyship may be in late," Coventry said. "I'm to see all is to her liking in the meantime."

"Of course, miss," the manager said. "Our house is honored, honored I say."

And so Coventry, who had begun the evening shackled to a hospital cot, ended it ensconced in the delicious, warm softness of a magnificent four-poster bed in one of London's premier hotels. Aside from her persistent headache, the uncomfortable truth that this hotel room was costing most of her limited funds, and the fact that London was crawling with coppers who wanted nothing better than to throw her in prison, she hadn't a care in the world.

Soon she was asleep.

Coventry rose to meet a bright, sunny morning feeling mightily refreshed. The fog had burned away and her head had cleared. She felt, as the Bard had said, bloody, bold, and resolute. She washed her face and hands, braided her hair, and went down to the dining room. She explained that Lady Winthrop had arrived at her room quite late and was feeling poorly. Therefore Her Ladyship would like her breakfast sent up to her room.

Coventry took delivery of the meal, as a good maidservant ought. She then enjoyed a capital feast of bacon, scones, an omelet, and fruit, eaten off silver dishes and washed down with beer served in a silver cup. She briefly considered taking permanent custody of some of the silverware, but decided it would invite trouble and let it be.

After breakfast, she set out in search of a dressmaker. She found an excellent, expensive one only a short distance from the hotel and went in.

"Begging your pardon, ma'am," she said to the proprietor. "But I'm here for Her Ladyship. That's Lady Winthrop, she's staying at the Grosvenor just up the way. She's needing a new dress, something as she can wear for a visit to Westminster."

"Oh, of course," the seamstress said. "We'll be glad to oblige. I'll just need her to pop in for some measurements and we can start putting it together."

"Well, here's how it is, ma'am," Coventry said. "Her Ladyship had a bit of an accident last night. One of her horses spooked at a stray cat and her carriage was overturned out in the street. She's all right, but she had a bit of a bump on the head and her luggage got all tossed about. The trunks split open right in the road, spoiled all her clothes but what she had on, and that was her traveling dress. So she's laid up back at the hotel, but seeing as how she and I are about the same size, she says it'd be all right if you just fit it to me. I wear all her cast-offs, ma'am, and they fit me wonderfully well."

The seamstress stroked her chin and looked Coventry over, already measuring her with her eyes. "I see. And this is something of a rush order, I take it?"

Coventry nodded vigorously. "Oh yes, she has a pressing engagement this very day, at noon sharp. This should be a fine dress, but Her Ladyship understands it mightn't be quite perfect. Just do the best you can."

"Hmm," the seamstress said noncommittally. "Well, we can but try. What's her color?"

"Blue," Coventry said promptly, having thought this through ahead of time. "Like a robin's egg, or the sky on a summer's morning out in the country. With maybe a bit of silver trimming."

The seamstress had her measuring tape out now and was moving around Coventry, taking her measurements with swift, experienced hands. "Will you be wanting a hat to go with this?" she asked.

"If there's time," Coventry said. "But if not, just a silver net for the hair should do well enough. Money's no object. It's only time that's wanting."

"I'll set my girls to work at once," the seamstress said. "I can have it brought to the hotel, if that will serve."

"Oh, that would be wonderful," Coventry said. "You can leave it at the desk for Lady Winthrop, or you can have it sent up to her room, if you please. And you can leave the bill at the desk."

"Of course," the seamstress said.

A short while later, Coventry set out from the dressmaker's shop. She then went to a women's shoe store and played the same game with them, ordering a pair of fine lady's shoes to go with the dress. Then she stopped at a few other shops and bought a few cosmetic items, including a comb and some makeup, and the most recent copy of *Debrett's Peerage*. Thus equipped, she returned to the hotel.

She spent the balance of the morning reading her new acquisition. This was no light pleasure-book. It was a record of every titled family in the British Isles, including how they were linked to one another by marriage. She'd paid little attention to such matters in recent years and felt she ought to bolster her knowledge. To pass as a well-connected society girl, she should know every eligible bachelor in the realm and be well-versed in the current gossip, especially who had married whom. It was dull and tedious going, but she persevered.

The shoes arrived at eleven. Coventry signed for them, knowing they would be charged to Lady Winthrop's entirely fabricated address. Lady Winthrop's bills would wander southern England like leaves drifting on the wind, endlessly accumulating and serving no real purpose. She tried on the shoes and found they fitted quite well.

The dress likewise arrived, in the hands of a breathless young woman. Coventry, feeling generous, tipped the girl a shilling in thanks for her promptness. Once she was alone again, she locked the door and tried on the dress.

The very feel of the fabric was marvelous, though the sensation was rather spoiled by the inevitable corset. Coventry looked at herself in the room's mirror, twirling the skirts about her feet. She saw a nineteen-year-old girl with pale skin and auburn hair, unusually pretty, with a fresh-faced innocence in her cheeks that did not match the haunted shadows hiding behind her eyes. She stared at a ghostly vision, at the echo of the privileged, naïve young woman she should have been, and promptly burst into tears.

"Stop it," she ordered herself. "Stop!"

When words did not suffice, she struck herself hard across one cheek, then the other, bringing a bright flush to her flesh. The stinging smacks restored her composure. She could not afford to indulge her self-pity. There was too much to be done. For one thing, there was the matter of her hair.

The best and most up-to-date hairstyles could not really be done to oneself. They were meant to be crafted by a lady's maid. Coventry did the best she could, working by feel, just as if she was picking a series of tricky locks. She braided and twisted, pinned and plaited. She held the whole complicated mass of intertwining braids together with several more strategically-placed pins, and laid a fine net of silver mesh over all. Then she looked at herself in the mirror once again, after steeling herself for what she would see.

She really did look quite lovely. No one who looked at her would see a back-alley harlot or pickpocket. She thrust her chin out defiantly and swept out of the room.

The clerk at the front desk smiled fawningly at her. "Good day, madam," he said. There was no hint of recognition in his face, though Coventry had walked past him earlier that very morning in other guise.

"Call a cab, if you please," she said, and her voice was not the rough cockney of Coventry Adams. Her accent was that of a pure upper-class blue-blooded lady. "For Lady Winthrop."

"Oh yes, my lady. Certainly. At once." He bustled off. The cab was waiting at the door only a few moments later. The cabbie helped her into the seat and she told him to take her to the

Houses of Parliament. Then she settled back to enjoy the ride, taking in the sights of well-to-do London.

She enjoyed the feeling of being dressed properly, eating well, being treated with deference. But none of it was real. It was all play-acting. It had once been her, but now she felt false. She wore so many masks. How could she say what her true face was? What voice was her own? What name?

The hansom pulled up at Westminster Palace. "Houses of Parliament, ma'am," the cabbie said. Coventry handed up his fare. Though she hadn't paid for her dress and would not, in fact, be returning to Grosvenor Hotel, she had still nearly exhausted her funds. But this man was not to know that. She gave him his coins lazily, with the air of one who had never needed to count pennies in her life. Then she alit from the hansom and walked toward the many-spired mass of Westminster Palace, surmounted by the massive tower of Big Ben. The clock's enormous face showed twenty minutes past noon.

Parliament was in session. That was good. Coventry hoped to take the opportunity to do a little prowling behind the scenes, which would be much easier without tripping over Lords and Commons at every step. The main thing was to discover what Bartleby Horrocks had been up to, so she needed to find his office. Perhaps she could share a few quiet words with the man's secretary, and then...

"Felicia?"

One could take a dog and retrain the beast, give it a new name, call it by its new appellation for years, and if one then called out its original name one day, it would bring up its head, ears perked, attentive. It would have no choice in the matter. Nor did Coventry. In spite of all her experience in matters of stealth and subterfuge, when she heard that name called in high-pitched feminine tones of disbelieving surprise, her head snapped around to look.

A black-haired, pretty young woman about the same age as herself stood a short distance away, staring at her with shocked recognition.

Chapter 8

*M*eredith, Coventry thought. *Meredith Waterston*. Of all the terrible luck, she would have to run into one of her childhood friends. She remembered Meredith as a sweet and charming if rather empty-headed girl, a year younger than herself. The Meredith of her memory was somewhat plump, her good-natured face framed by a bouncing mass of dark curls. Meredith had loved horses and the two of them had often gone riding together.

The Meredith who stood before Coventry had grown into a young woman. She still had a roundness to her, but her corset had squeezed and molded her into an attractive, even curvaceous shape. As Meredith recovered from her surprise, her eyes were alight with joy.

For a terrible instant, Coventry was sorely tempted to fling herself into the other girl's arms, to pretend the intervening years had not happened. She felt the pull back toward childhood, toward the illusion of security.

But she knew it to be an illusion. She put on one of her masks instead, a face of noble disdain leavened by a trace of confusion.

"I beg your pardon, madam," she said in her very snobbiest voice. "Were *you* addressing *me*?"

"Oh, Felicia, don't you remember me?" Meredith said, clasping her hands in front of her impressive bosom and bouncing up onto her toes excitedly. "I know I must look rather different, and you look quite different yourself. Your face, it's older, and your eyes... but you look lovely, quite lovely! Oh, we shall have so much to tell one another!"

The man at Meredith's elbow, a distinguished-looking gentleman in a very fine suit accented by a gold watch-chain and cufflinks, stepped forward and touched her elbow. "My dear," he said. "I take it this is an old acquaintance?"

"Hardly," Coventry said with a sniff that tore her heart on the inside. "This *young person* seems to have mistaken me for someone else. And whom might I be addressing?"

The gentleman swept off his hat and made a perfect bow. "Your pardon, madam. Leicester Snowbourne, baronet, and your obedient servant. This is my wife, Meredith. I fear I have not the honor of your prior acquaintance, Lady...?"

"Lady Winthrop," Coventry said, covering her surprise. Little Meredith was *married?* But that was not so very odd. She would be eighteen now, and it appeared she had made a good match. A baronet was not so high in social rank, but if this Leicester Snowbourne had money, as it seemed he did, things might turn out well for her. He looked to be in his early thirties at most, so the age gap was not as great as might be, he was neither grossly fat nor ugly, and he seemed polite. His eyes were kind, and that was a considerable comfort.

"Oh, you are married as well? How splendid!" Meredith said, doggedly refusing to be put aside. "I don't think I know Lord Winthrop, but you look very well. Only... how is it we heard nothing of your wedding? Nothing of you at all, come to that, ever since you vanished on that trip to London with your father. The police were involved. I remember, it was quite the scandal!"

"Sir Leicester Snowbourne," Coventry said, speaking clearly and distinctly over Meredith's prattling. "I commend your manners. I can only hope that, as your marriage is clearly but lately consummated, such manners will yet have time to rub off on your outgoing but rather presumptuous bride."

Sir Leicester winced and colored slightly. He coughed and took firmer hold of Meredith's arm. "My dear," he said in an undertone. "You are bothering the lady. Pray be silent."

"But she's *Felicia!*" Meredith exclaimed. "I know her! We were friends growing up! You know, the daughter of Lord Fox-Brooke? Don't you recall when she vanished? It was in all the papers!"

"My personal doings are never spoken of in the *London papers*," Coventry said, laying cold and contemptuous emphasis on the last two words. "I can only conclude this well-meaning but *overly familiar* young lady is attempting to embroil me in some manner of distasteful scandal. What her purpose is, I cannot guess, but out of charity I shall presume her intentions to be pure but misguided. Good day, Sir Leicester."

"Ahem, yes, my humble apologies, Lady Winthrop," Sir Leicester said, coughing politely. "Meredith, my dear, will you please be silent? You are insulting the lady and embarrassing me!"

Meredith's eyes welled up with tears. "Felicia?" she whispered, doubt finally clouding her face. "Don't you... don't you know me?"

Coventry, in answer, swept majestically past them and into Westminster Palace. She dared not linger a moment longer, or she might lose control of her masquerade. The look of anguish on her old friend's face was almost more than she could bear. But if Meredith were to know the truth, she would be unable to keep it to herself. She had always been something of a gossip and had already proven unable to hold her tongue. Half London would know before the week was out, and the other half by the end of the month. Her father would hear of it, and the whole story would come out. The shame would be unbearable. It might be the death of him.

The only answer was not only to deny Meredith, but to crush her so completely that she would not dare even to bring up the chance-meeting in conversation. It was a terrible thing to do to a friend, but Coventry had become something of a connoisseur of terrible acts these past years, and Meredith's pain would pass. The girl would convince herself she had imagined the resemblance and would be mortified at having offended a stranger, nothing worse than that. At least Coventry hoped so.

She paused inside the doors, heart pounding, and gave herself a moment to recover. The weight of the entire world, with all its judgment and power, hung over her head. Let her make a single wrong step and it would come crashing down and bury her.

Perhaps this was a fool's errand. Finn Farrell was already half-convinced of her innocence in Bartleby Horrocks's murder. She might be able to simply walk away, go back to the life she had carved out for herself.

But Coventry was a stubborn girl, not one to back down once she had set herself a task. She needed to see this through. She clenched her jaw, reminded herself to walk smoothly and with grace, and glided into the halls of Westminster.

She had been here in her past life, when her father had allowed her to accompany him to Parliament. She had been overawed by the sheer size of the place, the bustle of activity, the important men engaged in the vital business of the Empire. But that had been long ago. Now she saw only a great many self-important fools making much out of nothing. They moved bits of paper here and there, pretending they understood the world.

A footman directed her to Bartleby Horrocks's office, though he gave her a curious look and asked what business she had there. She answered his impertinence with such a withering stare that the poor fellow was reduced to a quivering jelly. She left him quaking in his shoes and went on her way.

The office was locked, which was fortunate. Coventry had prepared a story for the man's secretary, but was glad she need not bother. Lies had a way of piling up and getting in one's way. On the other hand, a solid brass lock now stood between her and her goal, but Coventry was not one to let something so trivial thwart her.

She cast a quick glance up and down the hallway and saw many men going about pointless errands. She attracted some attention, for there were few women present. She met the eyes of any man who dared stare at her, glaring haughtily until they turned away. Then, having conquered all comers, she turned her attention to the door.

If she had still possessed her lockpicks, it would have been child's play to gain entry. Two hairpins sufficed, but it took a dangerously long time. Her sole shield was that she was performing the act of breaking and entering so brazenly, in broad daylight with many folk around her, that no one suspected a thing. Thieves worked under cover of darkness, swathed in dark clothing. They certainly did not pick locks in Parliament while wearing fine light-blue dresses. Any observer simply assumed she was struggling with a stiff key in an uncooperative lock and took no notice. After an endless minute, the tumblers clicked into place and the office door swung open.

The first thing she did upon entering was to turn the bolt, locking the door once more. Then, free from interruption, she looked around. The office was neat and tidy, furnished in expensive hardwood. Coventry ignored the secretary's work area and made for Bartleby Horrocks's massive desk. Its drawers, too, were locked, but with very simple little locks.

She worked them open one by one. It was a fun little diversion, one she rather enjoyed. It reminded her of opening parcels on Christmas morning, being surprised by each new treasure. Granted, those parcels had held such things as scarves, mittens, dolls, and toys, while Mr. Horrocks's desk contained political correspondence, but the thrill as she opened each drawer was the same.

She skimmed over the documents, not even certain what she was seeking. The papers were dry and dull. Even the handwriting in the letters was stiff and stodgy. Bartleby Horrocks had been engaged in correspondence with many men in the Foreign Office. For all that these men were diplomats, they must have saved their flowery speech for dealing with foreign dignitaries. The letters Mr. Horrocks had received were decidedly terse in tone.

A particular letter caught her eye. Its handwriting was better than most, but its tone was, if anything, harsher.

———— ❧ ————

March 9, 1871

To: The Honorable Bartleby Horrocks
Dear Minister,

I received your letter of the 8th, detailing your concerns as to Russia's intransigence respecting the Black Sea, and her renunciation of those clauses of the Treaty of Paris pertaining thereto. Are you truly of the opinion that I am unaware of the significance of these developments? Perhaps, sir, you think me too timid in these matters, as you have hinted upon many prior occasions.

Do not, sir, confuse prudence and patience with timidity. It cannot have escaped your notice that France, lately humbled by the Prussian Army, is in no position to take a firm line with Russia. Her military is shattered, her ambitions thwarted, her head bowed in defeat. We can hope for no support from that quarter. Why do you think the Czar is so bellicose?

I am not a fool, Mr. Horrocks, and I dislike being taken for one. I know the Czar's ambitions all too well, for they reflect Russia's eternal quest: her lust to possess a seaborne trading route to the rest of the world. The Black Sea is her gateway and the Ottoman Turks hold the key at Constantinople. While the Turks hold the straits of the Dardanelles, Russia's watery dreams must suffer a rude awakening.

How is it that I must explain these matters to you, as to a child? Do you still intend to throw your ridiculous tantrum in the House of Commons and denounce this new agreement before the vote is called? Do you not realize that you will bring slander and ridicule not only upon yourself, but upon this whole administration? I cannot allow you to take such rash action. The consequences, should you refuse to be restrained, may be dire, and I shall not be answerable for them.

This is but one more move in the Great Game we have been playing against Russia, with Europe as the stakes, for the past forty years. God willing, we will still be playing it forty years, or four hundred years, hence. But you, Mr. Horrocks, have no part to play henceforth. You are dealt out of the game.

Go off! I discard thee!
Your Obedient Servant,
Lord Granville

Coventry sat back in Mr. Horrocks's comfortable leather chair and whistled softly. In the language of gentlemen, that letter could be construed as a threat. The Second Earl of Granville was the Foreign Secretary, the man most in charge of the Empire's diplomatic affairs. He was clearly in the midst of delicate negotiations with Russia regarding a treaty which Coventry vaguely remembered from her history lessons. As she recalled, the Crimean War, which had ended when she was still an infant, had mutually exhausted its participants—Britain, France, Sardinia, and the Ottoman Empire on one side, Russia on the other. Everyone had wanted that messy and fruitless war to end.

She tried to think what she knew about the peace agreement which had been signed in Paris in 1856. For the first time in her life, Coventry wished she had paid closer attention to international affairs. She did know that the British had taken the great city of Sevastopol on the Black Sea, and that to get it back, the Russians had needed to make serious concessions.

Now, apparently, Russia was feeling stronger and the Czar was seeking to expand Russian influence. That was doubtless of great interest to men like Granville, but not to Coventry, except insofar as it helped explain what had happened to Bartleby Horrocks.

Mr. Horrocks had been opposed to any new arrangement with Russia, vehemently so, to judge from Granville's testy letter. He had been intending to make a speech against a new treaty in the House of Commons. That speech would never be delivered, as Mr. Horrocks's lips had been permanently sealed.

There was the motive she had been seeking. But could she really accuse the Foreign Secretary? Lord Granville was a tremendously powerful and influential man. He was quite capable of having a man killed, should his aims require it. But had he done so in this case? And if he had, was she in any position to bring him to account?

Coventry's mind was spinning. She folded Lord Granville's letter and tucked it into an attaché case that leaned against the desk. On impulse, she scooped several other letters that looked to be of similar sort into the case as well. Then she searched the rest of the desk. In the top left-hand drawer she found a rough copy of Mr. Horrocks's speech. She decided to take that as well, and peruse it later. It might offer some additional hint as to why someone might wish to silence the troublesome Minister.

The attaché case was hardly a proper accouterment for a young lady. Coventry cursed herself for not thinking to arrange a handbag in advance. But it would have to suffice. In any event, it was high time to be gone. Mr. Horrocks might be dead, but his secretary most likely was not, and might show up at any moment.

She walked to the door, unlocked it, and opened it. She stepped boldly out into the halls of Westminster, spine straight, head held high. The only thing she had to fear was showing her fear, though hiding it proved more difficult than she had anticipated. She had only just realized that she was now holding a collection of official letters from a Minister of Parliament. If she was taken up now, it would not be merely as a murderer and thief. She would be considered a spy!

As she digested that disquieting notion, she saw a pair of high conical helmets moving above the heads of the crowd. Coppers, two of them, and coming toward her! They had not yet seen her, for the eyes of the men were well below the peaks of their helmets, and Coventry was small of stature, but they could hardly miss her bright robin's-egg blue dress, a lone splash of color amid a sea of suited dignitaries.

"Bloody hell," she muttered under her breath.

"I beg your pardon, madam?" said a startled-looking clerk at her elbow.

"I said 'very well,' sir," Coventry said. "And I hope I find you the same."

"Ah, yes, of course, madam," he said, smiling awkwardly. "Is there some way in which I might assist you?"

"I seem to have gotten myself rather turned about," Coventry said, speaking deliberately slowly, fighting down panic at the approach of the police. "This place is so very confusing.

Might I trouble you to direct me to the House of Commons? I wish to witness the debate regarding the forthcoming treaty."

"Oh yes, of course, madam," the clerk said. His smile grew more genuine and he bowed. "It would be my honor to accompany you."

Coventry took the hand he offered and they set out, thankfully in the opposite direction from the Bobbies. As they went, the clerk kept nervously babbling.

"Of course, you can't go into the House itself, madam. With the, ah, restrictions upon the, ah, fairer sex. As you no doubt know. We can't have delicate flowers being bullied about in the rough-and-tumble world of politics. But there's the attic, naturally. Twenty-five tickets per day. I assume you have your ticket?"

"Of course," Coventry lied stiffly, in the tones of one who thought herself slightly insulted. On the inside she was raging, against the stupid men who ran Parliament with its antiquated rules, but also against herself. The clerk was correct. She knew perfectly well that women were not allowed to visit the House of Commons or to sit in the gallery. But with all that had happened this past day, she had quite forgotten it.

The place reserved for female visitors to the House was very far from the beaten path in Westminster. Indeed, were it not for the unanticipated need to have a place where women could be neither seen nor heard, the attic would have been relegated to serve as an archive for the dusty minutes of forgotten sessions of Parliament. The clerk escorted Coventry up two flights of stairs to an unassuming little door with a small, neat man in front of it.

"Here you are, madam," the clerk said. He hung about with the air of an expectant dog.

"Thank you," Coventry said, but when no further thanks, either pecuniary or affectionate, were forthcoming, the clerk departed.

"You're here to listen to the debate, madam?" the man in front of the door asked.

"Of course," she said.

"And your ticket?"

"I have it about me," she said, approaching and rummaging in her case. The man's hand strayed to his coat pocket, which told Coventry everything she needed to know. She stepped in close and dropped her case, which thudded to the floor.

"Oh," she said. "How terribly clumsy I am!" She started to reach for it.

"Please, allow me," he said, gallantly and predictably.

"Oh, thank you ever so much," she said, touching his arm with her right hand as he picked up the case and straightened. Meanwhile, her left hand snaked into his pocket and plucked out a little scrap of paper. She concealed it between her first and second fingers as she took the case back from him with a smile. It was a standard pickpocket's maneuver. The best thing was to have a colleague provide the diversion, but in a pinch, she could use one hand to make contact with the mark while the other hand did the work. The target would notice the heavy touch and miss the lighter one nine times out of ten.

This was no exception. The man was neither surprised nor alarmed. Indeed, the touch of a pretty young woman's hand on his arm pleased him and distracted him marvelously well. Coventry went back to searching in her case. A moment later she smiled triumphantly and produced the ticket she had just purloined. She handed it over. The man bowed and stepped aside, opening the door for her.

The room within was furnished with a low couch and a handful of chairs. A group of women sat in these, clustered around a metal grate. Echoing out of the grate, like a voice from the underworld, came a male orator's sonorous tones.

One of the women, who looked to be in her mid-twenties, greeted Coventry with a warm smile. "Good day, madam," she said. "Welcome to our little circle. I do not believe we have had the pleasure of your prior acquaintance."

"Lady Winthrop," Coventry said. "And you are correct. This is my first visit to this... what shall I call it? Eyrie?"

"Oh, I rather like that," said one of the other women. "It could be a clever play on words. Do you recall Mr. Rochester's wife in the book? Bertha?"

"The madwoman in *Jane Eyre?*" the first woman replied, arching an eyebrow. "The woman who was locked in Thornfield's attic?"

"Precisely!" the second woman said with a merry laugh. "After all, is this not just what the Ministers wished to do with their unwanted women? Lock us all away upstairs where no one can see or hear the mad women with their unnatural political fixation?"

"You forget," the first woman said coolly, "that I am married to one of those same Ministers." She turned back to Coventry. "Millicent Fawcett, at your service. My husband is Henry Fawcett, MP for Brighton. And though he is one of those selfsame gentlemen, he is an ally in our noble cause, I assure you."

"Naturally," Coventry said, though she had no idea what cause Mrs. Fawcett might mean, and did not know her husband.

"And who is your husband, Lady Winthrop?" the second woman asked eagerly. "Is he in Parliament, too? I can't immediately recall a Lord Winthrop, but it is so hard to keep track of them all."

"No," Coventry said. "I am not married."

"Not married?" the woman replied in tones of astonishment. "But why ever not?"

"Hush, Celeste," Mrs. Fawcett said. "Lady Winthrop looks not a day older than seventeen. Besides, is not one of our purposes to ensure that no woman is wed before she is quite ready?"

"Just so," Coventry said. "Pray tell, what have I missed?"

"They're debating the Treaty," Celeste said. "Everyone was expecting a bitter fight in the Commons, but the whole thing seems to have rather sputtered out. The Lords have come out for it, of course, under Lord Granville's influence, and the Commons seem certain to vote in favor."

"But before the vote, we shall have to listen to many a man drone on and on," Mrs. Fawcett said, smiling cynically. "How men do love the sound of their own voices. Will it not be a fine day, Lady Winthrop, when one of our own speaks in the House?"

"As a Minister?" Coventry asked, startled.

"Obviously," Mrs. Fawcett said. "They cannot keep us out of their chambers forever, and once we are inside, it is only a matter of time before we win seats for ourselves. England is ruled by a queen, after all. The argument that we ought to be kept out of politics grows more ludicrous by the day."

Now Coventry understood. Millicent Fawcett was a Suffragette, one of those women who was agitating for the vote. Mrs. Fawcett naturally assumed that any other woman with an interest in politics sufficiently avid to bring her to this stuffy little room in Westminster must be a kindred spirit.

"It is ludicrous," Coventry agreed. "But we live in a land of traditions, Mrs. Fawcett, and changing them often requires a great expenditure of time and energy. I liken it to a project to divert the Thames into a new watercourse, or perhaps the engineering work on the new sewer system. It can be done, but will need much labor and will reshape the very land on which we walk."

"Well said!" Mrs. Fawcett said. "You see, ladies? We can speak as well as any of those learned gentlemen below, if we are once given the chance! Have I your permission to quote you, Lady Winthrop? I am in the practice of publishing booklets and pamphlets to educate our young women. Perhaps you have read my *Political Economy for Beginners?* I flatter myself it has reached a broad readership."

"A fine and necessary work," Coventry said, though she had never read it, nor even heard of it. She had been much too concerned with matters of everyday survival to pay much mind to the struggle for female enfranchisement. "You may feel free to use my words, but I must ask that you quote them anonymously. My family..."

"Say no more," Mrs. Fawcett said, nodding. "As a married woman and personal secretary to my husband, I enjoy greater autonomy than many young ladies, even those of noble households. Your confidences are safe with me."

"Hush!" Celeste said, holding up a hand. "They're calling the vote! Sooner than we thought!"

Coventry joined the circle of women and listened as the vote was slowly taken. It took a very long time, and she grew bored with the proceedings, but Celeste had a pad of paper balanced on her knee and was tallying the votes one by one. The ladies' rapt attention called to Coventry's mind the spectators at a horse race. She wondered whether there might be money to be made running a gambling book on Parliament. If so, she knew a few lads who might be interested.

"That decides the matter," Celeste said at last. "The Treaty is ratified."

"A victory for the Czar," Mrs. Fawcett sighed. "We shall be fighting another war within the present generation, mark my words."

"Surely it is also a victory for Britain," Celeste said. "After all, Lord Granville says—"

"Lord Granville is half fool and half poltroon," Mrs. Fawcett said crushingly. "He speaks as if the preservation of peace were always the most desirable outcome!"

"But surely, peace is eminently desirable," Celeste said.

"Not at any price," Mrs. Fawcett said. "There are things for which it is good, just, even necessary, to fight. The peace of submission is nothing more than slavery. Has not our sex learned this all too well?" She looked at Coventry. "What say you to that, Lady Winthrop?"

"I would die before I would be enslaved," Coventry said with honest feeling, only barely managing to stop herself adding "again" to the end of the sentence.

"British soldiers died taking Sevastopol," Mrs. Fawcett said firmly. "Our nation's greatest medal for heroism, the Victoria Cross, is cast from metal taken from those selfsame cannons our bold warriors captured that day! Today we have witnessed the betrayal of their memory, the negation of their valor and sacrifice. And for what? A few years of what we may laughingly call peace, while Russia rearms herself and fortifies her coast. How long before she feels herself strong enough and goes to war with the Turks? The Continent is uneasy, ladies, and this peace is a fragile and delicate thing. Though our sex does not fight upon the battlefield, it is our husbands and sons who will bleed for this day's sorry work."

"If only Minister Horrocks had not perished," said another lady who had not yet spoken. "He would have spoken out to stop the Czar."

"He should have known better than to consort with low women," Mrs. Fawcett said. "My Henry has informed me he was murdered by a harlot in a bed of sin. I may have been in agreement with Mr. Horrocks on some matters of international policy, but he was a loathsome man who received the just wages of his iniquity."

"It is quite certain that the harlot slew him?" Coventry asked. "I had heard someone else was present in his rooms."

"Henry told me the police were searching for a woman," Mrs. Fawcett said. "Perhaps this fallen woman has shown us something, my friends. Like Jael with General Sisera, she has exerted political power the only way she could. Our hands may be small, but they can be mighty. If we cannot wield the instruments of governance, perhaps we can still hold hammer and tent-peg."

Celeste shuddered. "You have the most awful ideas at times, Millicent," she said. "You are not advocating that women become *assassins*, are you?"

"It is hardly ladylike," said another woman.

"You might be surprised what a lady is capable of, when pushed to it," Coventry said thoughtfully. "But is it not a remarkable coincidence that the most vocal opponent of this treaty should be slain a mere two days before its ratification? A person of suspicious mind might consider alternative explanations for his death."

"Lady Winthrop," Mrs. Fawcett said. "You are a young lady of uncommon perspicacity and insight. I should take it as a great honor if you should call on me. Here is my card."

"The honor is mine," Coventry said, tucking the card into the stolen attaché case. One never knew when such an introduction might prove useful. "But now that the business before the House is concluded, I must take my leave. I have a pressing engagement."

The ladies all wished Coventry a good day. She departed the attic room with an unfamiliar feeling of warmth and goodwill in her breast from her meeting with these quietly revolutionary women. Perhaps her own crusade was not so hopeless as all that.

Chapter 9

oventry had a spring in her step as she left Westminster Palace. Granted, she still did not know who had killed Bartleby Horrocks, but she had considerably more information than she had possessed at sunrise. Then, too, Millicent Fawcett had enheartened her. After all, her opponents were merely men; dumb, brutish louts for the most part, slaves to their appetites. She had been outthinking and outmaneuvering men for the past two years, ever since her escape from Handsome Hal. They might be strong but she, Coventry Adams, was cleverer than they. Had she not just traipsed through the center of English government and out again, bearing a packet of secret papers, with no tools but her wits?

She had been basking in a warm glow of self-satisfaction for a few moments before she realized she was being followed by one of those men she had so recently scorned.

It was nothing she could lay her finger upon, but she felt a prickling on the back of her neck. Some instinct deeper than thought warned her that the man a few paces behind was not there by coincidence. How long had he been trailing her? Since Westminster, most likely, which did not bode well.

Coventry resisted the urge to look over her shoulder. That would only tell him she had marked him. She forced herself to keep walking in a smooth, ladylike glide. She could hail a cab, but that would not help her escape. It would only serve to trap her in a wooden box with no freedom of movement and several blind spots. No, it was better to stay on foot and keep her options open.

She silently cursed her fine new dress and new shoes. They were inarguably stylish and attractive, but her midsection was so pinched she could scarcely draw a deep breath and her feet were rubbed and chafed by the stiff, new leather. The thought crossed her mind that perhaps men wanted women to wear such clothing in no small part because it made them easier to run down and capture.

She continued forward, coming to a cross-street. A fine gentleman's carriage, drawn by four beautiful gray horses, trotted by. In the reflection of its clear, clean windows she caught a glimpse of the man who was following her. He was large, his face festooned with an impressive mustache. From the neck down he was dressed as an Englishman, in a fine suit and waistcoat, but his skin was a dark olive complexion and he wore a small cylindrical hat with a little tassel dangling from it. A fez, she thought it was called.

Why was a foreigner following her? Coventry did not know, but he looked like a rough fellow who knew how to handle himself. She started across the street, deliberately picking a moment when there was only a small gap between carriages. Perhaps that would delay him. She walked briskly, still seeking to keep up the façade of nonchalance.

As she reached the far curb, she saw another mustached, dark-skinned man closing in from her left. He was dressed identically to the first and looked so much like him that they might have been brothers. His hands were empty, which was good as far as it went. A knife would have been worse. But he was undoubtedly moving to cut her off.

Coventry turned on her heel and began walking to her right, just in time to see a third man running across the street some twenty feet ahead of her. She was boxed in.

The fear that rushed through her had not quite turned to panic, not yet. She was on a crowded London street, surrounded by her countrymen. Surely nothing could happen to her here. But she remembered with a crawling dread that just such a thing had indeed happened to her, three years earlier. Her father had been with her on that day, for all the good it had done. Now she was alone, helpless and unarmed.

Unarmed, perhaps. But never helpless.

A low voice, heavily accented, came from just behind her and to her right. "You come with us, please, madam," he said.

Coventry paused. She tightened her grip on the attaché case. "I think not, sir," she said, managing to keep the quaver out of her voice.

"You come quietly, yes?" he said, advancing. "Or we have something ugly on the street."

He reached into a pocket. His hand emerged holding a short, wickedly curved dagger. The other two men were very close now, flanking her on both sides.

These men wanted silence. They wanted her to come quietly. So Coventry screamed. She gave the scream all the breath her corset allowed, belting out a piercing shriek.

The sound was even louder than she had hoped. All three men drew back instinctively. But Coventry knew better than to count on sound alone to stop them. She had gained the briefest of advantages; that was all. She pivoted on her heel and shoved her attaché case straight at the man with the knife.

He reflexively stabbed at her. The blade was very sharp, driving through the side of the case. But two layers of leather sandwiched a thick packet of letters. The case was as good as a wooden plank and served as an excellent shield. Coventry saw the tip of the knife poke through the near side of the case, but it was only a pinprick. The blade was lodged firmly in place.

She twisted the case sharply. The man grunted and lost his grip on the knife. People were staring and pointing, most of the bystanders frozen in shock, but everything else was moving quickly now. The man on Coventry's right lunged at her, hands outstretched. She kicked him square on the kneecap with her hard leather shoe. His leg buckled and he went down, spitting a curse in a language she did not know.

The third man's arm came around her chest from behind, wrapping her in a tight embrace. His other hand clamped over her mouth. He held a cloth in it, soaked in some chemical. The smell was sweet and slightly alcoholic. Coventry gasped for air, sucking in a breath that felt cold and oily in her nose and throat.

A wave of dizziness assailed her. Her arms were pinned at her sides, but she was able to reach down. She groped behind herself and found what she was looking for. She grabbed and squeezed as hard as she could where the man's trouser legs met.

The man gave a deep, low groan of pain, but he did not release his hold. Coventry kept struggling. Pain pounded in her skull and the dizziness increased. She refused to give in, stomping on one of her captor's feet. His grip slackened a little, but that damnable cloth stayed over her nose and mouth, clouding her mind.

"I say, sir, unhand the lady at once!" an Englishman said. Coventry had a vague impression of snowy white whiskers and a black hat. She tried to speak, but only nonsensical mumbling escaped her numbed lips. One of the other two foreigners turned on the gentleman and struck him a heavy blow. The white-haired fellow toppled like a felled tree. Another woman screamed. Several voices called for the police.

The sounds were all blurring together. Coventry, in a last, desperate movement, flung her head back. She caught her assailant square on the nose. He released her and stumbled away, flailing and falling backward, blood squirting from his nostrils. The cloth fell away from her mouth and she sucked in a delicious gulp of fresh air. But her balance was gone and she, too, tumbled to the ground.

Strong hands seized her from both sides. She was lifted off the cobbles, still feebly struggling, and bundled into a dark room. The chamber bounced and jostled into motion. A carriage, perhaps? The thought swam aimlessly through her mind. Then another hand was over her face and the sweet chemical smell once more filled her nostrils.

"*Uyu*," a man said. He sounded very angry and out of breath.

It seemed to take a terribly long time to fall asleep, and Coventry fought as long as she could, but her thoughts and her movements became clumsier and more fitful. Her final efforts were pitifully weak. At last she fell away into a dark slumber too deep even for fear to penetrate.

Coventry woke gradually, swimming slowly upward toward light and consciousness. She knew, in some deep part of her memory, she ought to be frightened, and once awake, she certainly would be frightened again. It was easier to remain asleep, and in some odd way, safer. Like a child who buries her head beneath the blankets, she clung to the absurd notion that no harm would come to her if she kept her eyes closed.

Someone close at hand said something, but the words made no sense to her. They were just so much gibberish. Another man answered in similar nonsensical syllables. Coventry's head pounded. She wished they would be quiet and go away.

She started to move and found she could not. She could wiggle her fingers, but her arms and legs were held fast. She thought perhaps she was sitting up, which was odd. Something was holding her upright, some restraint around her chest.

"Ah, good. You are awake."

The man was speaking excellent English, but his accent was curious. His voice was thick and rich, reminding her of liquid honey. It held none of the rough cruelty of men like Handsome Hal. This man sounded well-educated, slightly amused, and interested.

Coventry opened her eyes. She was in a room whose walls were built of heavy blocks of mortared stone. No windows interrupted the featureless, undecorated stonework. The floor was smooth and hard beneath her feet. A pair of gaslights burned on either side of the room's only door, which looked to be made of iron. The effect was of an inner chamber in a medieval castle.

A man in a fine suit sat in front of her, one leg crossed over the other, hands clasped on his knee. He was slim and darkly handsome, a luxuriant black mustache adorning his face. He wore a very fine suit and expensive shoes. Another man stood in front of the door, arms folded, staring impassively at her. That man's face was bruised. His nose was crooked and clotted with dried blood.

At the sight of their mustaches and olive skin, Coventry fully recalled what had happened. She tried to spring to her feet and retreat from them. She could not move. She was tied to a chair. Ropes were tightly bound around her wrists, elbows, ankles, and breast. Panicking now in spite of herself, she thrashed wildly against her restraints. The chair-legs screeched on the flagstones. Then one leg caught in a chink between stones. The chair toppled. Coventry went over with it, crashing to the ground and banging her aching head.

"Ahmet," the man in the chair said, pointing to her. The man at the door immediately walked toward her. Coventry screamed wordlessly as he bent down and reached for her. She snapped at his fingers with her teeth, spitting helpless curses, half out of her mind with rage and terror.

"God damned son of a gutter whore! Filthy pigeon-livered meater! Ragbag gutter-dropped shite-head! I'll tear your throat out with my damned teeth!"

Ahmet, his face impassive, made no response to her incoherent threats. He took hold of the chair by its back, keeping his face well clear of her, and hoisted her upright once more. He went around behind the chair and held it in place. Coventry did not like this at all, the man's massive bulk at her undefended back, but he made no move to harm or molest her. Gradually, she managed to quiet herself.

"I say," the man in the chair said pleasantly. "My experience of Englishwomen is, I confess, quite limited, but I had not known them to display such facility in verbal abuse."

Coventry, face flushed, shoulders heaving from her useless exertions, glowered at him. "Come a bit closer and I'll give you an experience of an Englishwoman you'll not forget!"

"Come, come," he said. "This is hardly the behavior of civilized folk."

"Civilized?" she echoed. "Your hay-penny bully-boys snatch me right off the street and you've got the gall to talk of civilization? You, who's got me tied to a bloody chair? Take these ropes off me this instant, you damned coward, and then we can talk about civilization!"

"I think not," he said placidly. "My men are still recovering from their prior encounter with you, madam. Forgive me, but I do not know your name."

"I don't know yours either," she retorted.

"Ah yes, introductions. How thoughtless and impolite of me. I am Kadir Akman." He stood and actually bowed briefly and formally, as if they were meeting at a social function.

"Lady Amelia Winthrop," Coventry lied.

"Your accent and manner, forgive me, is not that of an Englishwoman of the upper class," he observed. "I know of no Lady Winthrop. Where is your family located?"

"Dorsetshire."

"Ah, of course," he said. "I shall have to review my copy of the *Peerage*. I must have overlooked the Winthrop family."

He and Coventry stared at one another for a long moment. Kadir smiled thinly.

"Well?" she challenged him. "Are you going to take off these ropes or not?"

"I will consider it when you begin answering my questions truthfully."

"Are you calling me a liar?"

His smile vanished. "Every woman is a liar, madam," he said coldly. "As is every man. Lies flow as readily from human lips as water runs to the sea. I know you are a liar, but even a liar can tell the truth when properly motivated. Please, for both our sakes, do so as speedily as possible. I have little liking for the sort of unpleasantness I must otherwise ask Ahmet to perform. But I assure you, he will do whatever I ask of him, with neither hesitation nor mercy. Recall, if you will, that he has no reason to love you."

Coventry swallowed. Kadir's eyes were very dark and completely serious. She saw now that he might be an educated and courteous man, but he was also a completely ruthless one. She began to be even more frightened. Her fragile bravado was cracking.

"Who are you?" she whispered.

"I have already told you," he said. "Now you will answer me. What is your name?"

She said nothing.

Kadir sighed. "Ahmet," he said, making another casual gesture with his finger.

Ahmet seized Coventry's hair down near the roots, twining his fingers through the strands to improve his grip. Then he began to slowly rotate his fist, twisting and pulling. The pressure rapidly changed to a thousand sharp points of pain. Coventry cried out, her eyes watering, and tried to get away. That only increased the pain. She saw stars before her eyes. He was tearing her hair out by the very roots.

"That will do," Kadir said mildly.

The pressure relaxed at once. Coventry sagged down, gasping for air, tears running down her cheeks.

"You see?" he asked gently. "This gives me no pleasure, I assure you, but Ahmet has thus far offered only the mildest of encouragements. Please, madam. You are young, not much older than my own daughters. Do not force me to hurt you. Ahmet will, if I ask him, drive splinters under your fingernails. He will tie wet strips of leather around your skull that will tighten as they dry and drive you mad with the pain, cracking your skull and popping your eyes from their sockets. He will flog the flesh from your back. He will harm you in unspeakable ways, in which only a woman can suffer. And in the end, you will tell me everything I wish to know despite your best efforts. So why go through this foolish resistance? What is your name, child?"

Coventry looked for mercy in his face and saw none, only a deadly purpose. She was confused. Every other cruel man she had met had enjoyed the cruelty, reveled in it. Kadir seemed entirely devoid of emotional interest in her plight. All he wanted was information.

"Which name?" she asked in a low voice.

"I beg your pardon?" Kadir said.

"Which name do you want? The one I was born with, or the one I've been using? I was Lady Winthrop this morning. Who do you want me to be?"

He smiled again. "Now we are getting somewhere. What name does your employer know you by?"

"I have no employer."

"Ahmet," Kadir said, lifting his hand again.

"No!" Coventry cried out. "Please! It's true! I work for myself, alone!"

"I do not believe you," Kadir said coldly. "You were seen leaving Minister Horrocks's office in Westminster Palace. You were carrying his private correspondence. A girl who looks very much like you was in his hotel on the night of his murder. You appear deceptively young and innocent, but you are a creature of the night, a spy and an assassin."

"For God's sake," she snapped in exasperation that almost overcame her fear for a moment. "I didn't kill the bloody bastard! Why does everyone think I did?"

"So you were there," Kadir said, nodding. "I thought so. You were spying on Minister Horrocks. For whom?"

"For nobody!" she said. "I didn't even know his name when he picked me up!"

"You expect me to believe this nonsense?"

"It's the truth! It's what I do! I gull gentlemen, drug them, and snatch their bees once they're out!"

"Their bees?" Kadir repeated. It was his turn to be confused.

"Bees and honey!" she translated impatiently. "Money! I'm a roller! A thief!"

"Ah," Kadir said. "So you robbed Minister Horrocks?"

"That's all I did to him! I slipped a bit of laudanum into his drink to knock him out, then I rolled him clean and took my leave. He was alive when I left him. I didn't stab him, I swear it!"

"Then why steal his documents from Westminster?"

"Because the bloody Bobbies think I killed him, same as you, and they're trying to pin it on me! I needed to find out who really did for the daft bastard, so I don't swing for it! What's it to you, anyway? You don't seem like great bloody friends of his!"

"Minister Horrocks was my friend," Kadir said. "And a friend to my people. His death is a great misfortune for us."

"That's something we've got in common," Coventry said bitterly.

"You maintain that you did not kill him?"

"Of course I didn't!"

"The letters in your bag pertain to the London Treaty, not to any murder. They do not prove your innocence. You are lying, madam. You are a spy."

"I am not!"

"I have heard enough." Kadir signaled his man once more. "Ahmet, go and heat your irons. We shall see if fire can burn away this woman's deceit."

"What? No!" Coventry looked at him with unfeigned fear. "You can't! I've told you the truth!"

"We shall see," he said. "Do try not to scream too loudly, little one, for your own sake. No one will hear you in this cellar, so it is quite useless, and you will not wish to render yourself incapable of speech by tearing out your own voice-box with your shrieks."

"No!" she screamed at him, abandoning all pretense and all dignity. "No! Please! I'll do anything! Anything! Don't hurt me! Just tell me what you want!"

Kadir got to his feet and walked to the door. Ahmet went with him. In the doorway, Kadir paused.

"When we return, madam, I will ask you one more time," he said. "I advise you to be more forthcoming."

He closed the door on her wordless wail of denial, leaving her alone with the echoes of her terror.

Chapter 10

For the next few minutes Coventry went, for all intents and purposes, mad. The pain, fear, and helplessness tore her loose from her internal moorings and swept her back to the terrified sixteen-year-old girl who had been abducted from a railroad station. The three years that had since passed were as nothing. The memories were as clear, sharp, and bitter as ever. Coventry Adams, the tough, streetwise façade she had constructed as a shield against the world, shattered. All that remained was Felicia Fox-Brooke; an innocent, foolish girl with no sense of the world.

She had gone into London with her father. He had some business matters to attend to regarding the estate, a dull subject in which she had little interest. But he was also buying horses. A breeder had brought several fine Andalusians over from Spain and Father wished to purchase a mare for his stables. She dearly loved horses and had begged him to come along. She had been so excited. It was a long journey to London and they rarely made the trip. She wore a new dress, blue silk, and thought she looked very pretty in it. Blue had always been her color, setting off her auburn hair most attractively.

Father stepped away, just for a moment, when they debarked at the station, and she lost sight of him in the crowd.

Then a serious-faced, good-looking man approached her. He told her he was with the police and she must come with him at once, that something had happened with her father.

Felicia never thought to ask to see his badge of office, did not even pause to question him. Awash with sudden dread, thinking of Father lying injured in the street, she followed the stranger like the trusting fool she had been.

It was not until he bundled her into the back of a coach with a hulking, grinning, foul-smelling lout of a man that she felt the first horrible doubts as to his intentions. She began to struggle and cried out for help. The only answer she received was a savage clout to the face that laid her out flat.

The fact of the blow had stunned her more than the pain of it. Nobody had ever struck her before. Father had always been kind and gentle, had rarely even raised his voice, let alone his hand. Felicia began to weep in confusion, fear, and growing hurt.

"Here now, Ned!" the handsome man snapped. "Don't go bruising the merchandise! How many times must I tell you, don't strike them in the face!"

Ned mumbled an apology. Felicia turned instinctively to the other man for protection. What an empty-headed ninny she had been. Handsome Hal Holcomb was no protector. His interests were solely commercial. Felicia had been right; she looked very pretty indeed, fresh-faced, innocent, and young. Those traits fetched a high price in the market he ran, the market of female flesh. A blackened eye or a crooked nose would hurt her value.

Still Felicia did not understand, not even when they brought her, blindfolded and bound, into a musty room at a foul boarding-house in the East End and tied her to the bed-posts by both wrists. She begged and pleaded with them not to harm her, as if she was dealing with men who understood mercy or kindness.

She had learned better. Harsh lessons, but necessary ones if she was to survive. And Felicia learned, slowly and grimly, hardening her heart, bearing what she must while she waited for her chance. There were moments of despair, but she endured them, always waiting for the opportunity she knew must come. No man could be vigilant forever. Handsome Hal would make a mistake. And when he did, she would be ready.

It took a year, an endless year in which she never left the boarding-house and rarely left that noisome, dreadful room. She was taken ill several times, but it was her fortune or curse to recover. She scarcely noticed what the men did to her anymore. She learned to detach herself, to hide deep inside where they could not find her.

And then it happened. A folding pocket-knife fell from the waistcoat of one of her "gentleman callers." Felicia managed to snare it with her toes and secret it away beneath her pillow. In the early morning hours, when the house had discontinued its business for the night, she caught up the knife in one hand, unfolded its blade with her teeth, and cut her bonds. Then she worked the tip of the knife in the door lock. She had not been good with locks, not yet, but she had an instinctive feel for it, and this lock was old and loose. She teased it open and hurried into the upstairs hall.

It was sheer bad luck that she met Handsome Hal at that moment, running square into him. But he was surprised and rather stupid with drink, so he was slow. Felicia was swift and desperate. Her first stroke laid his face open, the gash gaping so widely she saw the white of his cheekbone. Then, striking with all the savagery of panicked hatred, she had cut him again, across the brow, and a third time, splitting his chin, before he caught her up with both hands around her throat.

He began to throttle her, squeezing with all his strength while his blood streamed down his face and dripped to the floor. But Felicia still held the knife. She drove it into his eye until she felt the tip scrape bone. How he howled! He released her and she fled blindly into the pre-dawn darkness of Whitechapel, half-clad, bloodstained, and desperate.

She might have gone to the police, but when once she was finally free of Handsome Hal, the shame of what she had become overwhelmed her. She knew full well what sort of woman she was now. Fallen, disgraced, soiled, ruined. What good would it do to speak to the police? They would see her as scarcely better than Hal. And she could never go home. The shame would be too much for her, too much for her father and mother. She could never be married now, never take part in ordinary life. She would be nothing but a burden and a disgrace to her family. Far better they think her dead.

And so Coventry Adams was born in a back alley; an orphan, a true child of the streets. She had done what she must to survive and gradually she had clawed her way up. For two years she lived by the quickness of her wits and the lightness of her fingers, holding to two unshakable vows. She might be fallen, but she would not be damned. Whatever else she did, she would never take a human life. And she would never be enslaved again.

Now she sat, tied to a chair in a cellar, once more at the mercy of merciless men, and Coventry was truly terrified. Despite all her efforts and determination, she was trapped, enslaved, helpless. They would hurt her and then, when she was no more use, they would kill her. So she lost herself in an inner psychic scream of utter, despairing terror. Fear blazed up in her, blinding and consuming, until it finally burnt itself out to scattered embers.

When her wits returned at last, she did not know how much time she had wasted. Her wrists burned where the ropes had chafed them. Her throat was hoarse from screaming. Her eyes were red and her cheeks were wet with tears.

"Enough," she whispered, her voice cracked and pitiful. Kadir and Ahmet would return at any moment, bringing with them their instruments of torture. There was nothing she could tell them that would satisfy them. Kadir had already chosen not to believe the truth. It would do her no good if he finally believed her after she had been utterly broken in body and mind. She had long ago learned the bitterest lesson of all. No bold gentleman was going to ride to her rescue. Felicia Fox-Brooke could indulge herself in fantasies of being a damsel in distress. Coventry Adams had to save herself.

The first order of business was to free herself from her bonds. She had been trying to break them with main force. That was a stupid, panicky thing to do. She lacked the strength for such a feat. She must find the weakest point in her bindings and attack it, carefully and methodically. But how to manage that? She could not move.

But the chair could. And the ropes were strong, but they were dry. Coventry worked her feet along the floor experimentally. The chair slid slightly. She leaned her weight back, going up on her tiptoes as far as she dared, until she teetered at the very limit of her balance. Then she reversed her weight and flattened her feet, tilting forward.

She nearly overbalanced onto her face, but caught herself on the balls of her feet. Now she stood in an awkward half-crouch, still tied to the chair, which was delicately balanced on her back. Coventry walked in a tentative, tiptoeing shuffle toward the door. It took a terribly long time to cover the ten feet of floor that separated her from it.

Now she was next to the gaslight just to the right of the door. It was a simple design, just an iron bracket with a glass shell attached to it, within which flickered the coal-gas flame. Coventry chose her angle and leaned in, jamming the corner of the chair into the glass. It shattered with a faint tinkling sound, leaving the flame openly burning.

This was the dangerous part. But if she did not dare the fire now, she would soon face a worse heat. Coventry went up on the very tips of her toes, stretching as high as she could, and just managed to bring the rope into contact with the flame where it was wrapped around the chair. She held it as long as she could, but her feet protested mightily. Not even a trained dancer could have held the pose for long, like a ballerina on pointe. She sagged back, the chair clattering to the floor once more.

For a moment, she thought she had failed. But then she caught the scent of burning rope and knew the flames had caught in its fibers. She heard a faint crackling and felt heat at the back of her neck.

The chief danger was that her hair might catch fire. She was thankful she had done it up in braids that were wound about her head and pinned in place. Fortunately, it had not come loose in her previous struggles, though it had provided Ahmet with an unpleasantly convenient grip for his hand. She forced herself to be patient, to let the fire do its work.

Long moments passed. The smell of burning grew worse. Coventry wondered if the chair might catch fire. But it was hard wood, dense and sturdy, and did not readily ignite. The rope smoldered and smoked. Then the strands parted, one by one, and Coventry sagged forward, free from the waist up. The smoking rope fell away to the floor where it continued to burn. That was no danger; the floor was solid stone.

But her hands were tied with separate lengths of rope. She stretched her neck down, feeling her corset dig into her ribs. She needed only an inch more, perhaps less. By sucking in her breath and straining painfully, she was just able to close her teeth around the edge of the knot that secured her right hand.

After that it was just a matter of wriggling and tugging until one end of the knot unraveled. Then her hand was free and the rest of the knots were no more than a momentary concern. She stood and shed the ropes, stretching her aching limbs. She was certain her corset had bruised her side where the whalebone had jabbed her. But that pain was a small and inconsequential thing.

Now she faced the iron door of her prison. It was locked, of course. Coventry had never heard of a prison that was not. Kadir had taken the case which held Mr. Horrocks's documents. Doubtless he had also gone through her clothing in a search for weapons or tools. But that blind, foolish man had neglected to search her hair. Most likely he was more accustomed to dealing with male thieves and spies. Coventry still had her hairpins.

She went to work on the lock, reminding herself not to rush. A lock had to be teased, wooed, seduced. There were no shortcuts. The tumblers had to be tripped one by one. Her fingers did their accustomed dance, finding their way.

The lock clicked open. Coventry's hair now hung in a pair of braids down her back. She tucked the hairpins back into the braids near the top, knowing she might need them again. Then she pushed the door open, praying the hinges were well-oiled.

The iron squeaked. Her heart jumped into her mouth. But the door opened onto an empty hallway with a stair at the far end. She saw no sentry. From a doorway on her left came the roar of a furnace, which had drowned out the squeal of the iron. She edged to the opening and peered cautiously around the doorframe.

Ahmet stood with his back to her, facing the furnace. He wore long leather gloves and had several metal things that looked rather like fireplace pokers laid out on the edge of the furnace mouth. They were glowing a bright cherry red.

For just an instant, Coventry considered rushing the man and giving him a good, hard shove in the back. He would pitch forward into the furnace and that would be the end of him. But she could not do such a thing. She had made a vow. She stepped quickly past the door and continued toward the stairs.

The stairway led to another solid-looking door, this one made of oak. Coventry tested it and found it unlocked. She placed her ear against the wood and listened, hearing nothing. She drew it open as quietly as she could. Then she poked her head out, ready either to pull back or to dash forward as the occasion demanded.

She let out a sigh of relief. The hallway beyond, an elegant corridor of white stone, was empty save for a few alcoves which contained suits of outlandish armor.

Coventry needed a plan. Kadir had Mr. Horrocks's letters, but there was nothing she could do about that. He might have hidden them anywhere, or be carrying them on his person. They were as good as lost. Escape was the best she could hope for, and she would need to be fortunate to accomplish even that. She had no idea where she was, nor who her captors might be. Foreigners, obviously, but most of the world was made of foreigners. How long had she been unconscious? They might have carried her miles away.

She did not think so. Something, the taste of the air, the look of the building, told her she was still in London. The foreign embassies were clustered in Belgravia. That was her best guess, but she needed to get to a window, or preferably out onto the street.

She was obviously in some grand house or mansion. Such places had many exits. The cellar in which she had been held was probably accessed by a back stairway, so she thought she must be near the rear of the building. A kitchen door was likely nearest, and least likely to be guarded.

Coventry glanced in either direction, made a guess, and went left. The floor was polished marble and the hard soles of her new shoes clacked loudly upon it. She knew time was desperately precious, that her escape would soon be discovered, but she needed stealth. She stopped next to an alcove, ducked aside, knelt, and swiftly unlaced her shoes. She tied them loosely together and hung them from her neck. It was awkward, but she would want them once she was outside. She had experienced quite enough of London's cobblestones beneath unshod feet.

Straightening, she paused as the suit of armor caught her eye. A vicious-looking curved sword was clenched in the figure's hand. It shone brightly, forged of some marvelous type of steel that showed a dizzying pattern of whorls and swirls along its blade.

Coventry did not know the first thing about swords, but she knew a weapon when she saw one. It was the work of a moment to loosen the gauntlet's grip upon the scimitar. It was large and heavy for her, so she held it in both hands at waist height. Thus armed, she continued on her way, her stockinged feet making no sound on the floor.

The hallway branched off to the right and continued ahead. She paused, considering, and heard footfalls to her front. She ducked down the right-hand passage and ran, trying not to lose her grip on the awkward and unfamiliar sword.

She came to a gracefully arched double doorway which opened onto a large open space. A curving stairway led up on her right to a balcony. This was clearly the main entrance hall of the building. Rather than moving toward the rear of the house, she had blundered directly to the front door, the exact opposite of her intention. Coventry cursed inwardly. It was sure to be guarded. But perhaps she might find a way to slip out. She flattened herself against the wall and cautiously craned her neck to see what might stand between her and the door.

At that moment, she heard voices in the front hall. She recognized Kadir's cultured, accented tones.

"I understand your concerns, my young friend," he said. "But I must remind you, your feet stand on sovereign soil. Your authority does not extend to this building, nor to anything or anyone within."

"And I repeat, your lads were standing on sovereign British soil when they assaulted an Englishman and abducted an Englishwoman," the answer came.

Coventry felt a thrill of mingled surprise, fear, and unexpected relief at the second voice. Finn Farrell's Irish brogue was unmistakable. But what on Earth was he doing here? She leaned farther out into the hall, trying to catch a glimpse of the men.

Kadir was standing in front of the main doors, one of which was open. A man in an outlandish military uniform stood beside him, arms crossed, scimitar and pistol hanging from his belt. Finn was on the threshold, accompanied by a uniformed copper. The detective looked very angry. He was clutching his wooden truncheon in a white-knuckled hand. Two more of Kadir's foreign soldiers stood on either side of the policemen, rifles on their shoulders.

"That is a serious accusation," Kadir said. "I hope you can prove what you say."

"I can prove it in any court," Finn said. "I've the statement of the gentleman who was assaulted, along with at least a dozen witnesses. This man," he indicated the copper beside him, "Constable Bledlow, witnessed three men manhandle a young lady into a coach, which drove directly to this embassy."

"That's right, guv," the copper said. "Saw it with my own eyes, I did. Three bulky coves carried a wee slip of a girl in the back way."

"And how do you know she was an unwilling guest of the embassy?" Kadir asked.

"She was all limp and white in the face," the Bobby said.

"A faint, no doubt," Kadir said smoothly. "A frailty to which the fairer sex, alas, are too often disposed. I shall make inquiries. If such a young lady is on these premises, which is far from proven, I am certain the men of whom you speak merely meant to care for and revive her."

"This will be quickly cleared up, if I could just speak to the young lady in question," Finn said, taking a step forward. "Where is she?"

The large guard at Kadir's side shifted his weight and moved to bar Finn's path.

"A thousand apologies, Detective," Kadir said. "But your laws have no force here. This is Ottoman soil, by treaty and international convention. You may, of course, lodge a formal protest with the Ambassador, but you cannot enter without our permission. That permission, alas, is not forthcoming at this time. I must ask you to depart."

"You kidnapped a citizen of the Empire," Finn growled. "That's more than a matter for a formal protest, it's an act of bloody war!"

"Are you a soldier, Detective?" Kadir asked softly.

"I'm a member of the Metropolitan Police," Finn shot back. "And I'm doing my duty upholding the law and keeping the peace."

"In London," Kadir said, pointing at the floor. "But this is not London. This is Turkey. You know nothing of war. Are you truly prepared to risk a rift between our nations over something so trivial as a girl who may not even be what she appears to be?"

Finn froze. "And just how would you be knowing that?" he asked in a dangerously quiet voice.

"I know a great many things, Detective," Kadir said. "Which is why I am the one giving the orders here. Now I ask you once again to depart, before these men forcibly eject you."

"If you throw me out, I'll be back," Finn promised. "And I'll have the Queen's soldiers with me when I come."

Kadir was unimpressed. "These are diplomatic matters, not police matters," he said. "Leave them to the diplomats."

"And soldiers should leave war to the generals?" Finn retorted.

"A wise man knows when he is set to fight a losing battle," Kadir said.

"But I'm not a wise man, sir," Finn said. "I'm an Irishman. We don't know how to lose."

"Some would say that is all the Irish know how to do," Kadir said with a sneer Coventry could hear. Then he gave an order to the soldiers in their own language. The riflemen moved in, holding their weapons across their chests.

Coventry held her breath, waiting to see what Finn would do. Caught up in the drama at the door, she had momentarily forgotten her own situation. She was rudely reminded of it as a hand fell on her shoulder. She spun to see a man dressed in foreign garb and holding a tray in his other hand, upon which balanced a crystal decanter and several glasses.

He said something she did not understand, probably demanding to know what this English girl was thinking running about a foreign embassy in her stocking feet and waving a purloined sword.

Coventry let go of the sword with one hand and used that hand to knock the tray into the man's face. An almost comical look of dismay came into his eyes as the decanter tipped and tumbled, spilling water into his face. He released her and fumbled at the falling crystal, trying vainly to arrest its descent. It struck the marble and shattered with a remarkably loud crash.

A shout of alarm came from the big man at the front door. Coventry saw him looking directly at her. Kadir, too, was staring at her, eyes wide with sudden surprise.

The game was up, so she did the thing she thought they would least expect. She charged, waving her stolen sword and shrieking wordlessly.

Finn might be no soldier, but neither was Kadir. The Turk nimbly stepped behind the burly guard. That man, however, did not panic for an instant. He swept out his own scimitar and brought it up to a ready position. Clearly, he knew exactly what he was doing with the curved blade.

Coventry recalled something she had once read about sword-fighting. The world's best swordsman did not fear the second-best swordsman, but he did fear the worst. A terrible fighter would do unexpected, unorthodox things and was therefore dangerous. And Coventry was a truly terrible swordswoman, utterly untrained. Still shrieking, she flailed at the man's face, having neither the desire nor the expectation of hurting him, trying only to get him out of her way.

He neatly parried her wild strokes, batting her blade expertly aside with two swift, efficient movements. She was left wide open to his counterattack. However, the guard was not certain whether he ought to kill her. He wasted a moment in a sidelong glance at Kadir, who impatiently barked an order.

Then he turned back to her, no expression at all in his eyes. He bent his knee and lunged at her with his scimitar.

Finn's truncheon thrust neatly between his legs. The guard tripped, his feet hopelessly tangled, and fell flat on his face.

Kadir turned on the Irishman with a look of outrage stamped on his normally serene features. Finn offered him a lopsided smile and the slightest of shrugs, as if to ask what he had expected.

Coventry leapt forward, planting a foot directly between the shoulder-blades of the fallen guard, pushed off his prone body, and sprang past Kadir and through the doorway. Kadir saw the movement out of the corner of his eye and made a grab for her. In reflex, she lashed out with the sword she still held in her right hand. The edge of the blade whistled through the air, its very tip catching the man just below the eye. A fan of bright blood sprayed through the air and spattered the polished white marble.

Kadir fell back, clutching his cheek. Finn sidestepped and looped his left arm through Coventry's own, just as if they were a couple dancing. Her forward momentum turned into a circle around the detective, who led them in a retreat down the steps of the building and into the street. The two riflemen now held their guns poised and aimed, but hesitated to fire without orders. They knew, rightly, that to discharge their weapons into London would indeed be an act of war.

While the Turks hesitated, Finn and Coventry made good their retreat. Constable Bledlow, acting as rearguard, followed the other two away from the front door.

"Good evening, Miss Adams," Finn said in a pleasant, conversational voice, just as if they had met on a quiet stroll. "Fancy meeting you here. We do have the strangest habit of running into one another."

Kadir was leaning against the doorway, one hand clapped to his cheek, blood seeping between his fingers. "You will regret this, Detective," he hissed. "You have violated Ottoman soil! The Ambassador will hear of this outrage! You will lose your position!"

"I've had enough of this," Finn said in disgust, half-turning to face the angry Turk. "I never violated your bloody building, sir. Never crossed the threshold. And I'm guessing you don't want your precious Ambassador to know about this nasty business any more than I do. If it was official, you'd not be bothering with this cloak-and-dagger nonsense. So I think I speak for the entire British Empire when I say, sir, kindly feck off and good day."

Chapter 11

Coventry looked around, trying to place herself. They were definitely somewhere in London's upscale district. Her guess of Belgravia seemed accurate. She did not know it nearly as well as the lower quarters of the city, but she was confident she could quite easily lose herself, given the chance.

Finn's hand on her arm suggested he was thinking along similar lines. The detective was walking briskly, head constantly swiveling to take in everything, but his attention was primarily focused on her. He tucked away his stick and gently plucked the scimitar from her other hand. She did not resist.

"Half a moment, guv," she said. "I need to put my shoes on."

"Let's just get round the corner, shall we?" Finn said. "Constable, are they following us?"

"Not yet, guv," Bledlow said. "I shouldn't wonder but they'll be out in two shakes."

"I'm thinking the same," Finn said. He led Coventry left at the next intersection, putting a building between them and Kadir's embassy. "All right, Miss Adams. Tie your shoes. You've not got a knife in one of them, have you?"

"You having me on, guv?" she said. "I was a prisoner in there. You think they'd leave me a knife?"

"I'm thinking you were carrying a great bloody sword when I saw you," he said. "Screaming like a wee bonny banshee, you were, fit to curdle a lad's blood in his veins."

"A what?" Coventry asked, kneeling and swiftly tying her shoes.

"A banshee. It's a spirit we have in Ireland, the ghost of a wicked woman. She hangs about grave mounds and wails in the night. It's uncommon bad luck to hear one. They say if you hear the wail of the banshee, you or one of your close kin will surely die."

"It was bad luck for Kadir," Coventry said. She stood up. "Can I have my sword back now?"

"You're claiming this is yours?" Finn asked, hefting the blade. "It's curious. I was thinking this is just the sort of weapon a Turk might be carrying, a scimitar of good Damascus steel, but it's an odd one for a London lass. I'd best hold onto it for the present, given you pulled a knife on me yesterday."

"Sorry about that," she said.

"I'm sorry I struck you so hard. How's the head?"

"It'll mend."

"Grand." Finn waved to a passing hansom, which pulled up. "Hop in, Miss Adams. You and I are going for a wee ride. Thank you for your help, Constable Bledlow."

"Just doing my duty, guv." The copper touched his helmet and sauntered off.

Coventry considered bolting, but Finn was still watching her and she hesitated. Perhaps she was simply tired of running, but when he offered his hand to help her into the cab, she took it and climbed in.

"Where to, guv?" the cabbie asked.

"Where are you staying?" Finn asked her.

That was not the question she had been expecting. "Nowhere, at the moment," she admitted.

"Westminster Palace," Finn told the cabbie.

"Right you are," the man said, and they were off.

"Why there?" Coventry asked.

"That's where you were taken by the Turks," Finn said. "It seems only fair to go back, in case you've any unfinished business thereabouts. And you're welcome."

"For what?"

"Saving your life."

"I saved my own life," she said, bristling. Then she saw the slight smile on his face and relented a little. "But thanks all the same."

"Now, I imagine we've a few questions for one another," he said. "Starting with what each of us was doing at the Turkish Embassy."

"They didn't give me much bloody choice," she said bitterly. "The bastards nicked me off the street, clapped a rag over my face and threw me in a carriage. I'm thinking they dosed me with chloroform, the filthy swine."

He nodded. "That's what the lads said had happened. Do you know who these fellows were?"

"Turks?" she guessed.

"Aye," Finn agreed. "Agents of the Ottoman Empire. Not the Ambassador, nor his men, I'm thinking. Spies."

"Bloody spies!" she spat. "And now they think I'm one myself!"

"Why would they think that?" he asked. "Because they think you killed Bartleby Horrocks?"

"Everybody thinks I killed Bartleby Horrocks," she said wearily.

"I don't."

She stared at him. "Really?"

"I think you're a liar, a thief, and a cheat," he said, his smile widening. "I know you've slipped police custody twice in the past two days. You've given me a rare beating and led me a merry chase. You've also set fire to a hospital. What the devil were you thinking, doing that?"

"I was thinking I needed a diversion," she said, returning the smile. She liked the twinkle in his midnight eyes. "Besides, I didn't set fire to anything. It was your man did that, coming into the room all careless-like. And you left me tied to a bed. What sort of gentleman does that?"

"The sort who's possessed of some knowledge of the sort of lass he's dealing with," Finn said. "And I clearly didn't tie you tight enough. But I'm sure now you didn't kill Horrocks. And so I apologize for ever suspecting you."

Coventry gave him a suspicious sidelong look. "What's your game?" she demanded. "You've been chasing me all over this bloody city, and now you say the whole thing's pointless?"

"I'm saying nothing of the sort. I didn't follow you to the Horrocks house, I certainly didn't follow you to the Houses of Parliament, and the only reason I came to the Ottoman Embassy was I thought you might be needing my help!"

"The day I need a copper's help is a fine bloody day!" she snapped.

"Miss Adams, please," he said, laying a hand on her arm. She flinched away from the contact. Finn looked startled, then hurt, then concerned, the expressions flitting rapidly across his face one after the other.

"I never asked for your help," she said sullenly.

"But perhaps we can help one another," he offered.

"How?"

"Help me catch the killer," he said. "I've a description from the lad who took the statement at the hotel. But I need to know why Mr. Horrocks was killed. I assume it has something to do with the Turks."

"And the Russians," Coventry said.

"Russians?" he repeated. "Who said anything about Russians?"

"I think it's to do with the Treaty," she said. Seeing blank incomprehension on Finn's face, she tried, "The one they voted on in the Commons today? About the Black Sea? Sevastopol?"

"Miss Adams, I've no earthly idea what you're talking about. I steer well clear of politics. All I'm trying to do is solve a murder."

"But this murder's all about politics!" she said. "The dead man was an MP. He was going to give a speech in the Commons today to try to stop the Treaty. That's why they killed him!"

"How do you know that? Did he tell you when you and he, ah..." Finn's cheeks flushed slightly.

"Stop talking nonsense," she said, having no time for his prudishness. "This isn't pillow talk. I saw some letters between him and the Foreign Secretary. I thought maybe they meant Lord Granville had him killed."

"You're thinking Lord Granville had a Minister murdered?" Finn looked very skeptical.

"If you'd seen the letter..." she began.

"Where is this letter?"

She sighed. "The Turks have it."

"You stole the letter?"

"The Ottomans bloody stole it!"

"From you?"

"Well, yes..."

"And so you must have also stolen it first."

"That's hardly the point. The point is, I haven't got it anymore. They do! Along with Mrs. Fawcett's card and everything!"

"Who's Mrs. Fawcett and what's her place in all this?"

Coventry brushed the irrelevant questions aside. "None of your concern. We just need to figure who stood to gain by shutting Horrocks up."

"Anyone in favor of this Treaty of yours," Finn said. "And that includes the Russians?"

"Especially them. They're the ones who were pushing for it. And Lord Granville's going along with it to keep the peace. He thinks if the Government doesn't sign this treaty, there'll be another war with Russia, and the French won't come in like they did last time, so we might not win."

"Russians," Finn said thoughtfully. "The lad at the hotel said the man who complained about the noise was a big, black-haired fellow, a bit unkempt, with a black mustache. Heavy features, he said. That could be a Russian agent, I suppose. He gave his name as Dmitri."

"Sounds Russian to me," Coventry agreed.

"Or Greek," Finn said.

"So there's bloody Greeks in this, too?"

"The Greeks don't get on so well with the Turks, so it's possible," he said. "On the subject of the Turks, I'm worried that they kidnapped you."

"That's sweet of you to say," she said.

"You're very welcome, but that wasn't quite my meaning. As I told that lad at the Embassy, snatching an Englishwoman in London is an act of war. If word of it gets out, it'll cause a real donnybrook. They wouldn't do that unless they were desperate."

"They're scared of the Russians," Coventry said. "If Russia rebuilds their fleet in the Black Sea, who do you think they'll be using it on?"

"The Turks," he said, nodding. "They're willing to risk a little war now if it stops a bigger one later. You're right, this is all political. Bloody hell. If I'd wanted to get mixed up in political murders, I'd have stayed home in Ireland."

"Got a lot of those back home, do you?"

He smiled again. "You've no idea."

The cab stopped moving. "Here you are, guv," the cabbie called down. "That'll be nine pence."

Finn handed up a sixpenny bit and three pennies. The cabbie pulled his lever and opened the door. Finn climbed out and offered a hand, which she took. The cab drove away into the afternoon streets.

Coventry looked at Finn. "Well?" she asked. "What now?"

"I believe you," he said. "But I'm not the only copper in London. They've put the word out on you. You're still wanted for the murder. I'm supposed to take you in."

"But you didn't clap me in irons," she said.

"I tried that already," he reminded her. "I could try it again, but what's the bloody point? You'd be out of them before I'd time to draw breath."

She grinned. "So you're not arresting me?"

He shook his head. "Maybe some lad will haul you back to the Yard in chains, but I'll not be the one to do it. Not today, at least. Have you a place to go?"

"Don't worry about me, Finbar Farrell," she said. "I'll get by. I always do."

"Please, it's Finn to my friends," he said.

She arched an eyebrow. "Is that what we are now?"

"Aye, Miss Adams, I'm thinking maybe we are."

"Friends don't hit each other on the head with sticks," she said.

"You've not known many Irishmen, I take it," he said.

"Well, if it's friends we are, then you can call me Coventry," she said.

"Coventry, then," he said. "Where can I find you if I need you?"

"I can't tell you what I don't know," she said. "I'll look you up. And I wouldn't worry. We do seem to keep running into one another. How did you know it was me at the Embassy?"

His smile lit up his whole face. "I didn't, but when I heard a pretty lass with reddish hair had got herself in a spot of trouble, I made an assumption. I'm having a thought, Miss Adams... Coventry, I mean. It's teatime, near enough. How would you like to go for a bite with me?"

She genuinely considered it. Then she shook her head. "Better if we don't, Finn. If we're seen together, it might not look good for you. Besides, your wife might find out you're consorting with low women."

He blinked and his cheeks went a remarkable shade of pink. "I haven't any wife. And I wasn't talking about consorting of any kind! How could you think such a thing?"

"I like seeing you blush," she said, giving him a wink. "Never met a copper who blushed before. Mostly your faces only turn red when you're yelling. Be seeing you, Finn Farrell."

Coventry considered her next move. Her resources were quite limited. Once again, she was down to the clothes on her back, with not a penny to her name. The Ottoman agents had thoroughly emptied her pockets. She supposed she ought to be grateful they hadn't stripped her naked while they were at it.

"He might at least have left me the sword," she muttered, watching Finn's back as the detective walked away. "I could've sold it." Her stomach growled, reminding her it was tea-time and that she really should have taken him up on his invitation.

"Why didn't I?" she wondered aloud. "It's not like me to turn down a free meal."

Pride was a large part of it, she supposed. She might be a thief, but she was damned if she was a charity case. She could look after herself. But the truth was, she liked Finn. In spite of everything, she liked him. He was pleasant-spoken, canny, brave... and a copper who'd hit her on the head and tied her to a bed. Best to keep away from him.

In truth, her work was done. Finn knew everything she did. He seemed a competent sort, possessed of the necessary determination to see the job through. All she needed to do was sit back and wait for things to sort themselves out. If she could just keep out of the coppers' way, all would be well.

With that load off her mind, already feeling much better, Coventry set off to rebuild her capital. The cafés around Westminster were thronged with Ministers and their wives, mistresses, and secretaries. Coventry angled for men in the company of attractive young women. In the absence of a partner in crime, she found the other women useful as diversions. She approached her man of choice flirtatiously and familiarly. When he grew flustered and started to bluster, he invariably turned his attention to his companion, who was filled in turn with suspicion, jealousy, or confusion. While they nattered at one another, Coventry draped herself over the man and smoothly divested him of the contents of his pockets. Then, with an awkward apology for having mistaken him for somebody else, she begged off, leaving a gorgeous row in her wake.

Three repetitions of this tactic saw her finances replenished sufficiently to buy an excellent afternoon tea in a different café than the one in which she had performed her sleight of hand. Fortified by a delicious plate of buttered scones, a fine white cake, and two cups of tea, she next visited a dress shop, where she purchased a plain green dress and hat with a matching handbag. She then hailed another cab and went back to the East End.

The cabbie was uncertain of this, asking whether a fine lady like herself really ought to be going there. He was well-meaning and perfectly correct, but Coventry gave him a short answer, distracted as she was by the difficulties of changing clothes in a hansom without wantonly displaying herself in its windows. She managed this, though there were a few touchy moments in which any gentleman who happened to glance into the hansom as it trotted by would have gotten quite an eyeful. It was necessary, however. To walk about Whitechapel in her fine blue dress without escort would have been an invitation to robbery and assault. While she was at it, she pinned up her braids once more and covered them with her new green hat.

She dismounted two streets over from her old haunts. The cabbie blinked incredulously when she climbed out of the cab wearing entirely different clothing than when she had gotten in. Then he shook his head and drove his horse onward, only too glad to get out of the neighborhood before dark.

Coventry moved through the gathering dusk, walking in the manner she had long ago learned. Her step was firm and confident, her ears tuned to any untoward sound from the alleys. She took refuge in the crowds of poor Londoners, knowing she was unlikely to be accosted in the presence of so many others. Armored in anonymity, she made her way to Fergie's rag and bottle shop.

The dusty, dim environs of the shop closed around her like the familiar arms of an old friend. A pair of seedy-looking characters were lounging near the front window, but Coventry paid them no mind. Fergie was behind the counter, looking nervous and unkempt as ever. When he saw her, his eyes bugged out.

"Watch it, Cov," he hissed. "There's grasshoppers asking about you. Thick as fleas, they are."

"I know," she replied in a low voice. "Ran into an inspector on the way. Don't worry, Fergie. I'm clean. It's all been sorted."

His eyes darted toward the men at the window. "That's as may be, lass. But there's some within call as would sell their dear mums for a song, and from what I hear, there's guineas for the lad who hands you in."

"Thanks for the tip," she said. "I'll be fine and dandy."

He shook his head. "You're not hearing me. All sorts of lads have been through. And not just the coppers, neither. There was this Irish cove, dressed like a dock-hand, but too clean by half..."

"Black-haired chap? Young, bit of a dash on his lip?"

"That's the one, aye."

"I've an understanding with him. He's a copper, but he's all right for all that."

"What about the husky cove, the big swarthy chap?"

Coventry frowned. "What husky cove?"

"Great big lad," Fergie said. "Hairy. Rough-looking. Asking questions about a lass looking like you. Didn't know your name, though."

"When did you see him?"

"Not half an hour past. He's gone now. I told him naught, goes without saying. But you'd best be about your business and on your way, Cov. Crossroads of the bloody world, my shop is today." He spat disgustedly on the floor. "Nobody buying anything, neither. What is it you're wanting?"

"A lady," she said, looking him straight in the eye. "And a drum."

Fergie whistled low. "You sure about that? If you get nicked carrying that sort of thing, it's transportation for certain."

"I've been facing the rope, Fergie," she said. "You think they'll care if I'm carrying iron? How many times can they hang me?"

"Your funeral, love," he said. "Half a moment. I don't keep that manner of thing up front."

He disappeared into the back room. Coventry, feeling eyes on her, turned to regard the men at the window. They stared at her. The one on the left chuckled and grinned, showing rotten, stained teeth. She stared back and bared her own teeth. Still chuckling, the man left the store. His companion followed him out.

Fergie returned bearing a grease-stained rag. He glanced around the store, verifying they were indeed alone. Then he unwrapped the rag to reveal a small pistol, the "Lady from Bristol" she'd asked for.

"Lefaucheux pinfire revolver," he said in a conspiratorial whisper. "Belgian, just came over from the Continent. Twelve-millimeter barrel, metal cartridges. This is what they're carrying in the French Navy these days. One of those lads got drunk in one of the taverns down by the docks the other night, lost track of this little toy."

"Cartridges, too?" Coventry asked. She knew little about firearms. Most of what Fergie was saying meant nothing to her.

"Oh aye," he said. "How many are you wanting?"

"Enough to load the thing." She carefully picked up the pistol. It felt very heavy in her hand, cold and dangerous. She set it hurriedly down.

"Six, then," Fergie said. He hoisted a leather pouch and flipped back its flap to reveal a neat array of metal bullets, close-packed. They reminded Coventry of a devilish honeycomb.

"How much?" she asked.

"Fifteen quid. Including the bullets."

"That's too bloody much!"

"Like you know the first thing about irons and what they cost, Cov. These are hard to come by and dangerous to keep!"

"Then I'm doing you a favor, taking it off your hands. I'll give you twelve."

"Fifteen," he repeated. Then he shrugged. "You said you're wanting a knife, too. I'll throw in a good blade at no charge."

"Done." She handed over most of the money she'd taken off the men at the café. "But you'll need to load the thing."

"You don't know how?"

She shook her head.

Fergie sighed. "All right, Cov. But be careful with this. You don't want to go blowing your pretty little foot off." With surprisingly skillful hands, he swiftly loaded six bullets into the revolver's cylinder.

She watched him with interest. "Were you a soldier, Fergie?"

"Once on a time, I took the Shilling," he said. "Worst mistake of my life. I was lucky to get out again." He spun the pistol around and extended the butt toward her. She took it with a certain reluctance.

"It's single-action," Fergie continued. Seeing her incomprehension, he explained, "You need to pull back the hammer, here, before you pull the trigger. Every time. Else it won't fire. You mustn't forget. And this is important, Cov. Don't ever point this at any lad you don't want to put in the bloody ground, or any part of yourself you're not prepared to lose. Pistols have a nasty habit of going off, will you or no. And if you try to bluff a lad and he calls, you're in a world of trouble."

She nodded and tucked the revolver into her handbag.

Fergie gave her a tight smile. "I'm only doing this because I like you," he said.

"I know, Fergie." She gave him the warmest smile she could under the circumstances.

"I'm guessing you want a knife that's good for sticking?" he asked.

"That's the idea."

He handed her a long-bladed, nasty-looking knife much like her old stiletto. "Here. And don't ever say I'm not soft-hearted."

"Thank you kindly, Fergie. You're a dear."

"Stay sharp, Cov. And watch your step."

The shadows had grown long and dark when she left Fergie's shop. The street was even more crowded than before as some of the longshoremen finished their shifts on the docks and went in search of refreshment. Coventry set off for Slinky McGee's. She had no intention of staying there. If Finn had been able to find her at Slinky's, other searchers could, too. But Finn wasn't looking for her at the moment and Slinky would know a place she could lay her head.

She was careful to check behind her before entering the alley that led to the gambling hall. She'd been ambushed more than enough times. But she saw only the usual Whitechapel denizens, living out their wretched lives.

There was a faint *meow* from behind a rubbish heap. Coventry stopped short.

"Whisper?" she called quietly.

A pair of glass-green eyes flashed at her from the shadows.

She folded her spare dress over her arm, dropped to her knees, and held out her hands. Slowly, coolly, as if the idea had just struck him, the black cat stalked out to meet her. He butted his head into her hand and rubbed against her. At the familiar feel of his warm fur, she had to blink back sudden tears.

"Oh, Whisper," she said, scooping up the cat in her arms and cuddling him close to her breast. "However did you get all the way back here?"

His purring sent delightful shivers through her. The cat made no reply, nor had he any need to give one. London was his domain, its back alleys his highways. He came where he chose and went when he pleased. Now he was back with the only woman he'd ever known to be kind, so he was content. And perhaps, later, she would find him something to eat.

"Very well," she said. "I won't be staying here, but if you want, you can come with me. No doubt whatever boarding-house I find won't be sorry for a good mouser."

She stood up, still holding the cat, and climbed the stairs to Slinky's door, her handbag dangling from one arm along with her spare dress. She shifted the cat awkwardly to her left hand so she could reach the doorknob.

Slinky did most of his business in the evening hours, when workingmen were looking for a way to rid themselves of their wages. His house was usually crowded by six o'clock and stayed that way until the wee hours. Coventry stepped inside, expecting the normal hubbub of men playing at cards and dice.

The room was dead silent. Coventry saw Slinky, behind his bar with its array of cheap bottles of rotgut. His face was pale and strained. She saw a number of other patrons she recognized. All of them were seated around the tables, but no games appeared to be going on. Every eye was turned toward her.

A very large man, hairy and with enormous shoulders, took a step toward her. "I know you," he said in heavily accented English.

"Well, I don't bloody know you," she retorted. "And I don't care to. Step off. I'm here to talk to Slinky."

"Coventry," Slinky said in a near-whisper, darting his eyes to the side.

She followed his look and saw Nick, the bouncer. The burly man was seated in his chair next to the door, but his head was slumped down on his chest and his face was covered with blood. Another stranger stood beside Nick's chair. He was holding a knife in one hand.

"Dobryy vecher," the knife-wielding man said. His smile was wolfish.

Chapter 12

"Sorry to disappoint," Coventry said. "But I've no notion what the devil you're saying. I don't speak whatever heathen babble you're spouting."

The large man came around the counter and advanced on Coventry. "He wishes you good evening," he said. "He does not speak your tongue. I do. I think we talk a little, yes?"

"I don't talk to blokes who point knives at me," she said, keeping an eye on the other man. If she bolted for the door, she didn't think she would make it out before he caught her. Whisper, in her arms, had stopped purring. The cat was attentive to the change in her mood and had become wary and watchful.

"When I see you before, I think you are just *prostitutka*," he said. "And the police are looking for you, yes? So why do you go to houses of government? What do you have from Minister Horrocks? What do you take from his office?"

"Who says I was there? Who says I took anything?" she retorted, taking a step closer to the door. The man with the knife closed in. He was nearly close enough to stab her.

The big man shook his head. "We do not watch you," he said. "But we watch Westminster. We watch Turks. We have many eyes. You come out of Turkish Embassy with policeman. Why? You work for the Turks?"

"For the last time, I'm no bloody spy!" she spat. "The Turks think I work for you, you think I work for the Turks, the coppers haven't the first idea what I'm doing, but nobody believes I'm just me! On my own! If you'd stop chasing your damned tails for one bloody minute and look around you, maybe you'd figure some things out!"

The big man paused a moment, considering. Then he shook his head again.

"No," he said. "You come with us now."

"So you can lock me in another blooming cellar and break out your fire pokers? Not bloody likely, Dmitri, or whatever your blasted name is!"

He blinked and Coventry realized she had made a serious mistake. "You know things, little liar," he said. Then his eyes shifted to the man with the knife. "*Yuri, skhvatit' yeye za ruku!*"

Coventry had been tensed for fight or flight. She did not understand the words, but she guessed their meaning plainly enough even before Yuri lunged at her. His knife was still in his hand, but he was reaching with the other hand. They wanted to take her alive.

That knowledge gave her a very slight advantage. She intended to make them work for their prize. With a silent apology to her friend, she threw Whisper full in the charging man's face.

The alley cat had not expected this, not from the woman he trusted. He gave an earsplitting screech of outrage and twisted in midair, legs splaying out. He struck Yuri head-on. The startled man batted at the cat. It was an unwise move. Whisper flexed his paws, extending his claws. Even as he gripped Yuri's collar with his hind feet, he raked the man's face with his forepaws.

Yuri's hand struck the cat heavily. Whisper dug in his claws in an attempt to hold on. His sideways motion tore deep furrows in Yuri's cheek and across his eyelid. Then Whisper lost his hold and tumbled through the air, skidding across a table and scattering gambling patrons, none of whom wanted to be in the path of the spitting, wrathful whirlwind of fur. The cat fell from the table, landing neatly on all four feet on the floor. He scooted under the table and crouched there, bristling and hissing.

Yuri screamed and dropped his knife, clapping his hand over his injured eye. Dmitri growled a curse in Russian and ran toward Coventry.

She dropped her spare dress, shoved her hand into her bag, and snatched at the first thing she found. By good fortune, her fingers closed around the butt of her pistol. She brought up the revolver and pointed it at Dmitri, setting her back against the wall. Remembering Fergie's instructions, she used her other hand to pull back the hammer. There was a metallic click as the pistol cocked.

"Not one more bloody step!" Coventry snarled.

Dmitri froze. Yuri, still holding one hand over his eye, crouched down and groped for his discarded knife. One of Slinky's patrons kicked it away. The blade skittered into a corner.

"That's close enough," Coventry said. She felt behind her for the doorknob. Her heart was hammering in her breast. She tried to hold the pistol steady and wondered what she would do if Dmitri went for her. She could not, would not kill a man.

"You will not kill me," Dmitri said, as if reading her thoughts. He was looking in her eyes. Now a faint smile crossed his heavy, brutal features. "You are no killer. I have killed men. You? I think not."

"First time for everything," she said, pulling the door open.

He took a step closer, silently daring her to shoot. And she knew she could not do it, could not kill him. Worse, she knew that he knew it.

But Handsome Hal had long ago taught Coventry that there was a very wide space between life and death, and that space could be filled with pain.

Dmitri took another step toward her. She saw his muscles flex slightly as he prepared to spring. She lowered the barrel of the pistol. He smiled.

She pulled the trigger.

Coventry had never fired a pistol before and was utterly unprepared both for the tremendous noise and the vicious recoil. The revolver leapt in her hand like a rearing stallion, nearly tearing itself from her grasp. She went momentarily deaf from the terrific report of the shot. A cloud of thick smoke billowed into the air. The acrid smell of powder flowed up her nose and pasted itself to her tongue. She felt more than heard the vibration of a heavy body falling to the floor.

Through the smoke she saw Dmitri trying to rise to his feet. One foot trailed behind him, blood spattering Slinky's filthy floorboards. To her own surprise, she had actually hit what she'd aimed at; the bullet had punched through his foot. The Russian was bracing himself on the edge of a table. With his other hand, he fumbled out a savage-looking curved knife.

Coventry fled, running down the alley stairs and back the way she had come. Her eyes were watering from the powder smoke and she could scarcely see. A pair of blurred shapes loomed up at the alley entrance.

"Here now, love," one of them said, taking her arm. "Where be you a-going?"

She recognized the man with the foul teeth from Fergie's shop. In the same flash of recognition, she knew beyond doubt that he was working for Dmitri and that he had gone straight from the shop to tell him about her.

She savagely twisted her arm free and rammed the barrel of her revolver into the base of his throat. The man staggered back, choking and gasping in shock, his eyes big as saucers. His comrade, who had started forward to help, turned and took to his heels, running for all he was worth.

"I'll blow your windpipe to bloody rags, so help me," Coventry panted. Her eyes were wild, her hair disheveled. She had failed to convince Dmitri of her lethal sincerity, but she was much more persuasive now.

"Please, no," the man whispered weakly, shrinking away from her.

Coventry gave him another hard poke with the revolver barrel, making him cough. He fell against the wall and slid down the bricks to huddle in a whimpering, pathetic ball on the cobblestones. She left him there, shoving the pistol back into her handbag and hurrying into the Whitechapel streets. Soon she was gone, without even footprints to mark her passage.

Coventry was several streets away from Slinky's place before her thoughts began to fall into recognizable order. The loss of her fine new dress was a small thing. She had gotten and lost so much money and so many clothes these past days that they made little impression on her now. More serious was the presence of Dmitri and his henchman.

She did not trouble herself overmuch as to why he was pursuing her. It was enough to know that he was, and that either he or Yuri, possibly both, had killed Bartleby Horrocks. And they knew she knew Dmitri's name. That meant they would kill her, too, without a moment's hesitation. She was in deadly danger. And that was not even taking into account Kadir and his cronies, who would also be searching for her. They, too, would gladly torture and kill her. How had she managed to make enemies on every side of this absurd diplomatic conflict?

Where could she go? She had but two choices now. She could flee London altogether, make for the Continent, and hope to leave her pursuers behind. But that meant a life of constant uncertainty, looking forever over her shoulder for pursuit. And London was the city she knew, the one in which she had learned to survive. She would stand out in Paris or Madrid or Rome. Besides, the Ottomans and the Russians would have agents in any city to which she might flee, and they would not forget her.

Coventry's other choice was plain. She needed to make a plan, take the fight to her enemies, and defeat them. No matter how she tried to avoid acknowledging it, she needed an ally. Only one man in the city had believed her and helped her, in spite of the many ways she had ill-used him. Finn Farrell was the man she needed.

"I don't need any man," she protested angrily. As a general principle, that was admirable. Millicent Fawcett and her Suffragettes would doubtless have applauded it. But there was a time and a place for everything.

Now she only needed to find him. When she had airily dismissed him, she had not really expected to call on him again, especially not so soon. She had no idea where he lived, nor what his daily habits might be. Like her, he had been ranging the length and breadth of London. The only place she knew he would be was...

"Oh, no," she said aloud, drawing a curious look from a bystander. "Not there, Cov. Whatever are you thinking?"

It was an utterly mad idea, which was the beauty of it. It was bold, brazen, and not quite as dangerous as it appeared on the face of it. She just needed to change clothes one more time. The hour was growing late, but she still had time if she hurried.

"We're closed," the dressmaker shouted irritably through the door.

"Oh, no," Coventry said, her voice breaking a little. "No, please. I know just what I need. I'll only be a moment. I... I need something black. Do, do be kind, please? One woman to another?" In case the appeal to common womanhood proved insufficient, she held up a gold guinea against the window.

After a moment, she heard the bolt slide back and a wrinkled, frowning old woman opened the door.

"All right, get you in," the woman said. "A mourning dress, is it?"

"Yes," Coventry said. "For my... my father. He's just passed, quite suddenly, and I haven't anything to wear for the... the..."

"There now, dearie," the woman said, her frown dissolving. She patted Coventry's arm. "That's hard, but it's the way of the world. Just lost my own husband last month. Fine man, but the gin did for him. Poor Hubert never could leave a bottle unfinished." She sighed. "We'll get you fixed up right and proper. What were you thinking of?"

"Black silk, if you can," Coventry said. "With a crape veil."

"The usual thing, eh?" the dressmaker said. "Well, you're in luck, dearie, though perhaps I shouldn't call it that, considering. I have a dress I made for a young lady who lost her child. But then she didn't stop bleeding, and before she could take delivery, they were laying her out, too. She was just about your size. I think with just a little nip and tuck, on account of you being so thin... Yes, I do believe that might do. I'll fetch you a cup of tea while I work, there's a good girl."

The woman took some measurements, then gave Coventry a cup of what proved surprisingly good tea and went to work taking in the dress. She worked swiftly and skillfully, and in less than an hour the mourning dress was ready. Coventry tried it on, including the veil, and nodded her satisfaction at what she saw in the mirror. The woman in black who stared back was unrecognizable.

She traded her green dress to the dressmaker to pay part of the cost, using up almost all of her remaining funds to make up the balance. She wore the mourning garb, making sure the veil screened her face. Then, thanking the older woman with artificial tears, Coventry went out and hailed a cab.

"Scotland Yard, please," she said in answer to the cabbie's question. Her few bob would be enough to see her there.

Chapter 13

The fog had risen again and the sun was well down by the time Coventry dismounted in front of the headquarters of the Metropolitan Police. It was a stolid brick structure flanked by gaslights. A pair of uniformed Bobbies stood outside the front door, swathed in dark-blue capes.

"Evening, madam," one of them said, his hand momentarily emerging to touch his helmet brim before retreating back to its warm sanctuary beneath his cloak. His compatriot politely held the door for her. Coventry went in, wondering with amusement what he would do if he ever learned he had displayed such chivalry to a wanted fugitive.

Inside, the police station was well-lit and warm. A fire burned on the grate and several gaslights illuminated the interior. Though the workday had ended for most Londoners, the night shift of criminals, prostitutes, and vagrants was only beginning, and so the coppers were awake and alert. The place was a beehive of organized activity.

Coventry made her way to a desk behind which sat a gray-haired copper with a fine mustache. She acted hesitant and demure, as befitted a young lady in mourning.

"Evening, madam," the copper said. "Help you with something?"

"Please, sir," she said, using her posh upper-class accent. "I need to speak with Detective Farrell."

"What's this about, madam?" He looked at her sternly, but not unkindly, taking in her garb.

"My name is Esmeralda Horrocks," she lied. "My... my father was... was taken from me recently. The... the Honorable Bartleby Horrocks. Perhaps you have heard about it?"

"Ah, yes," he said. "Terrible business. Didn't know he had a daughter. My condolences, madam."

"Detective Farrell has been very kind," Coventry went on. "He was at my home last night. I had hoped to speak with him about his investigation. I have thought of something that might be of some small assistance."

"Oh, of course, madam," the copper said. "It's just that Mr. Farrell isn't often in. He moves all over the place, comes and goes as the mood takes him. Half a moment and I'll see if he's about the place. If you'll just sit yourself in one of those chairs, I'll be right back."

Coventry obediently sat, folding her hands in her lap. She watched the coppers going about their business for a few minutes. One wall was papered with broadsheets advertising rewards for the apprehension of criminals. With morbid fascination, she scanned these until she saw one in the lower right-hand part of the wall. It screamed for attention in large block letters:

POLICE NOTICE
£250 REWARD
Warrants have been issued against

Coventry Adams,
Generally known as
Coventry or Cov
For Feloniously Murdering the Honorable Bartleby Horrocks,
Esq., with a Knife, for the Purpose of Robbery; and also for Pros-
titution, Lewd Acts, Theft, Assault upon an Officer of the Peace,
and Felonious Arson, in which she set a Hospital Ablaze.
She is from 17 to 19 years of age, 5 ft. 1 in. in height, has a pale
porcelain complexion, red-brown hair of considerable length,
blue eyes, speaks with a Cockney accent sprinkled with vulgar
terms and profanity, and is given to hurling verbal abuse.
She is likely armed with a Knife and is considered Dangerous.
Lt.-Col. SIR EDMUND HENDERSON, COMMISSION-
ER, Metropolitan Police

Coventry suppressed a very unladylike snort at the description of herself. Two hundred and fifty quid wasn't half bad. For that sort of money, she'd consider turning herself in, if she'd only be allowed to keep it.

The gray-haired copper returned to the room, trailed by Finn. The Irishman looked much as he had when last she'd seen him; rumpled and weary, but still sharp.

"Esmeralda Horrocks, Finbar Farrell," the copper said by way of introduction.

Finn darted her a swift, keen look. "Miss *Horrocks*," he said. "If you'd be so kind as to step into my office, we may speak more comfortably there."

She followed him up two flights of stairs. He led her into a room that contained three desks, but no other coppers at present. The moment they were inside, he closed the door and turned the lock.

"Finn," she said, casting her veil aside. "It's me."

"I know that!" he snapped, crossing the room in three swift strides and seizing her by the shoulders. "What the devil's in your head, coming here? Have you any notion how much danger you're in?"

She trembled in the face of his sudden outburst and the rough way he had seized her. Torn between lashing out and collapsing in terror, she did neither. "Yes," she whispered. "Please let go of me."

He looked down at his hands as if noticing them for the first time. "Sorry," he said in a much quieter tone, letting go of her and stepping back. He cleared his throat awkwardly and brushed his hands down the front of his coat. "That was ungentlemanly of me. Please, forgive me. I'm speaking out of concern for your welfare."

The veil fell back across her face. She adjusted it with shaking hands. "Finn, they tried to kill me," she said.

"The Turks?"

"No. Russians, I'm thinking. Dmitri and Yuri."

"Dmitri?" he echoed. "You mean the same Dmitri who reported you at the hotel?"

"How do I know? I didn't see him there."

"When did this happen? Where?"

"It might have been two hours ago. Slinky's gambling hall. That's the place—"

"The place we first met," he finished for her. "Aye. Two hours. Damnation! The blighter might be anywhere by now! Couldn't you get here any faster?"

"I needed a disguise," she said sharply. "I couldn't very well prance in here with my face on display. You've a poster with my description downstairs, in case you didn't notice!"

Finn ran a hand through his hair. "Aye, you're right, of course," he said. "Forgive me again. But we must find this man! He's the key to the whole business!"

"He ought to be easy to run down," she said. "Just follow the drops of blood and look for a big hairy man with a limp."

For the first time in the conversation, Finn smiled. "Left your mark on him, did you?"

She nodded. "Put a hole in his foot," she said. "He'll live, unless he gets blood poisoning."

"That's likely enough, dragging an open wound through Whitechapel. Nay, chasing him won't answer. He'll have got to a carriage by now. He's probably at the Russian Embassy, where we can't touch him. They'll never admit to having him, of course. He might as well be in Moscow, or on the moon!"

"Finn," she said, reaching out and touching his arm. "Can you protect me?"

"I don't know," he said softly. "I'll try, you've my word, but with assassins running about London, I just don't know. What did they want with you?"

"They were watching the Turkish Embassy. They know I was there. They're sure I'm a spy."

Finn's shoulders shook slightly. Coventry was alarmed, thinking he might be having a fit, until she realized he was laughing quietly. Then she was annoyed.

"You're so many things, lass," he said. "I wonder, have any of us the right of it? Or are you pulling the wool over my eyes, too? I shouldn't wonder at it. No blame to you if it's so, and no matter. If I can bring Dmitri here, I can have the lad from the hotel identify him. Then I can hold him. But so long as he's at the Embassy, he can't be arrested."

"So you need to bait him out," she said.

"Aye," he said doubtfully.

"For that, you need something he wants," she went on.

"You have a plan?"

"You have me," she said. "He'll come out if he thinks he can get me, especially now I've hurt him. Men are easy that way. Prick your pride and slap your face and you all lose your bloody minds. It's like baiting a bull to make him charge."

"Ever seen a bullfight?" he replied. "My understanding is, sometimes the Spanish lad gets a horn in his guts. This is dangerous. For you."

"It's more dangerous to leave him be," she argued. "You want him for the murder, I want him so he'll be no more threat to me. Tell you what I'll do. I'll go to his damned Embassy and fetch him out for you. I swear, he'll chase me."

Finn laughed again, louder. Then he stopped and his face changed. "Good God, you're serious."

"I broke out of the Ottoman Embassy," she said, shrugging. "How much harder can it be to break into the Russian one? I'll get in there, have a look about, and make some noise. I'll make sure he sees me. Then I'll scarper out. He'll follow and you'll be waiting with your lads to pounce on him."

"That's your plan, is it?"

Coventry nodded.

Finn shook his head. "And you're asking me to protect you? Are you plain barking mad?"

"I don't think so. But I'm scared, Finn." It was the first time she'd admitted that to anyone since slashing Handsome Hal's face.

"And you think if you do this, you'll not be scared anymore?"

"I'm not such a fool," she said. "I'll always be scared. But not of Dmitri. Finn, Kadir was going to torture me. They tied me to a chair in their cellar. They were heating branding irons in their furnace."

Finn's eyes hardened. "I'll remember that, should I meet him again, away from his precious bloody Embassy."

"If I help you beat the Russians, won't it tell the Turks I'm not their enemy?"

He nodded slowly. "Aye, it just might, at that. Two birds, one stone."

"Three," she corrected him. "Because it'll get your lot off my back, too. Here's the bargain. I get you the man who killed Horrocks, you get your lads to tear up my warrants."

"You set a hospital on fire," he reminded her. "You robbed a Minister of Parliament."

"An MP who was stepping out on his wife, looking for the youngest girl he could find walking the street," she snapped. "He deserved what he got and we both know it."

"Did he deserve to die?"

"I didn't bloody kill him!"

"You drugged him. He was helpless when the assassins came for him."

"As if being awake would have done him any bloody good!" she scoffed. "Horrocks was a fat, useless lump of flesh. Dmitri and his pal Yuri are killers. I'm lucky they didn't kill me."

"How did you escape from them?" Finn asked suddenly. "Hardened killers that they are?"

"I threw a cat at Yuri and shot Dmitri in the foot."

"You've a revolver?" His eyes widened.

"I had one when I shot him." That was true. He didn't need to know she still had it.

"I thought you weren't a murderer."

"That's why I shot him in the foot instead of the head."

"A lad can die from a bullet in the leg."

She shrugged. "The world's a dangerous place. I do my best to keep everyone breathing, but they were coming at me with knives. I was holding a bloody cat. What was I supposed to do?"

Finn chuckled again. "I hope the cat forgives your using him as a projectile."

"So do I." She smiled at him. "So what do you say, Finn Farrell? Do we have a bargain? What do you say about throwing this alley cat right in their bloody faces?"

He extended his hand. "It's a bargain, Coventry Adams."

She took his hand. "Don't fret, guv," she added with a sly smile. "It'll be worth your while. But I'll need a bit of help."

"What do you need?"

"Cab fare, or a ride to Belgravia. Buying this dress, and taking the cab to the Yard, left me skinned to the bone."

That was how Coventry ended up riding in an omnibus with Finn and half a dozen grim-faced coppers. Two of these were Finn's fellow detectives, both armed with revolvers in addition to the truncheons carried by all London coppers. Finn had explained that the mysterious veiled lady in black was an informant who would deliver a murderer to them. There was a certain amount of skepticism, coupled with a gentlemanly suggestion that perhaps the lady ought to sit this one out, but he overruled the objections.

"What're we doing in Belgravia?" one of the detectives wondered aloud when the omnibus pulled up near Chesham House, just down the street from Belgrave Square Garden. "Murderers don't spend their time in the diplomatic quarter."

"War's naught but the continuation of diplomacy by other means," Finn said quietly.

"Says who?" the detective demanded.

"Some Prussian lad," Finn said. "Name of Clausewitz. Fought in the French Army under Napoleon, I think."

"Bloody Frogs don't know the first thing about war," the second detective said. "Look what just happened to them."

"I trust you refer to their recent defeat at the hands of the Prussians, sir?" Coventry inquired sweetly. "Perhaps Detective Farrell and Mister Clausewitz have a point. Diplomats are nothing more than well-dressed, polite murderers."

"Hardly a diplomatic observation, madam," the detective replied, drawing a murmur of laughter.

"Now, we need to do this quietly," Finn said. "The young lady will obtain entrance to yonder Embassy. We're not to move until she comes out with our lad. Be careful, lads. This isn't the only Embassy hereabouts, and if we go ruffling the diplomats with noise and confusion, there'll be a rare headache in Westminster come morning. Quick and quiet's the game. Just because you've guns doesn't mean you need to be bloody well using them."

"We'll have you carrying one yet, Farrell," the first detective said. "Every copper will have them in the future, mark me."

"My shillelagh's always been plenty for me," Finn said, patting his truncheon affectionately.

"Bloody Irishmen," the second detective muttered. "Always looking for an excuse to knock heads."

The omnibus rattled to a halt. Coventry hopped down to the cobbles. Finn accompanied her.

"Are you ready and willing to do this, Miss Adams?" he asked.

"It's a bit late to be asking a question like that," she said. "But waiting won't make it any better."

Finn leaned in close to her. "Good luck, darling," he said softly. "If you need help, sing out and I'll do what I can, even if it means a diplomatic donnybrook."

"That's sweet of you, Finn," she whispered. "But I can take care of myself." Then, on impulse, she went up on her tiptoes and kissed his cheek. "You're not a bad-looking fellow, Mr. Farrell. But you really should put a beefsteak on that shiner you've got."

"You mean the black eye you gave me?" he replied in an undertone. But he was smiling. "Be seeing you."

Coventry began to walk across the street toward the Russian Embassy. Fog swirled around her, caressing her with damp, chilly tendrils. She glanced over her shoulder once. The coppers were already lost in the misty night. Up ahead, the glow of a gaslight drew her on. She reached into her handbag and extracted her pistol and knife, tucking them into her dress's sash. Then she took a deep breath, adjusted her veil, patted her braids to make sure her hairpins were in place, and went on.

Chapter 14

Coventry was glad of the fog. It wouldn't do at all for the coppers to see what she was about. Walking right up to the front door would have been stupid, not to mention suicidal. Her first obstacle was the wrought-iron fence ringing the Embassy. This was primarily a decorative line showing the edge of the Embassy's property, not a serious barrier, and she surmounted it with a quick, unladylike scramble. Not for the first time, she silently cursed the skirts required by her sex. Men did not know how well they had it with their trousers. But if a Victorian lady were to display her legs so wantonly, the poor men would scarcely know what to do with themselves. Riots and chaos would be the inevitable outcome.

She landed between the fence and Chesham House. The house itself loomed before her, a shape she sensed more than saw through the fog. Swiftly, in case anyone had heard her, she stepped forward and flattened herself against the wall. No one raised the alarm. She heard not a sound. She knew there were bound to be sentinels, but they would be at the doors. A window was a better way in.

A quick inspection told her the ground-floor windows were covered by iron bars. Clearly, the Russians did not share Scotland Yard's confidence in the safety of Belgravia. However, while the bars prevented easy entry at ground level, they also provided a convenient ladder by which she might reach the upper floors.

Coventry saw, just above her, a bay window jutting out from the wall. Smiling to herself at the figure she would cut should anyone spy her, she tucked the hem of her dress into her sash. This freed her legs for climbing, but also showed not only her ankles, but her stockinged legs above the knee; a more brazen display than if she had been wearing her red satin tart's dress. She spat on her hands, yet another unladylike gesture, and took hold of the window-bars.

The bars were securely affixed to the stonework and did not so much as squeak under her weight. She climbed to the top cross-brace. Then, balancing on her toes, she drew her knife with her left hand and took hold of the brace that supported the bay window. This forced her to lean back over open space, terribly conscious of the wrought-iron spikes atop the fence. If she slipped and fell from her perch, she stood an excellent chance of impaling herself.

By reaching up, she was just able to touch the windowpane. The window was closed. The absence of light through the curtains told her the room beyond was empty. She sincerely hoped that was true, because she would be unable to perform her next act silently. She thrust the blade of the knife through the thin space at the base of the window. It was a tight fit, and she had poor leverage, but by wiggling the blade back and forth she was able to ease it under the sash.

In Coventry's experience, most people were not overly cautious about locking their upper-story windows, and the Russians were no exception. The sash was closed, but it had not been latched. By twisting the knife on edge, she was able to force the window open to the breadth of two fingers. It made a scraping sound that seemed terribly loud to her, but the fog had a damping effect on noise and London's streets were full of odd sounds. No one else took note.

Her feet and hands were growing weary. She released her grip on the knife and eased her right hand through the opening she had created. Then she shifted her weight to that hand, gripping the windowsill, and retrieved her knife with her other hand. The sash immediately descended onto her knuckles, but it did not fall far and the pain was not bad. She tucked the knife between her teeth for temporary safekeeping. Then, feeling quite piratical, she shoved her other hand through the narrow gap as well. At that moment, her foot slipped and she swung out into space with a muffled gasp.

There she hung by her fingers, directly above the fence spikes. She was committed now. She must go up, or fall and impale herself on the fence. She let herself dangle a moment, gathering her strength. Then she pulled and flexed her arms, hauling herself up.

She rose slowly, so slowly. Her head reached the level of the window, then her shoulders, then her waist. At last, she was able to lock her elbows straight. She got some small purchase on the stonework with the tips of her toes. Then, gritting her teeth, she placed all her weight on her left arm and pulled up on the sash with her right.

The window did not budge. Her muscles strained. Her left arm began to tremble from the exertion. She bit down on the knife in her teeth and pulled with every ounce of strength she had.

With a sharp squeal of protesting wood, the sash abruptly flew up. Coventry fell more than lunged over the sill, tumbling through thick curtains to land in an undignified heap on the floor. The sash, unsupported now, slid back down like a guillotine, descending with a crash that Coventry thought might well wake the dead.

"Could've just rung the bloody doorbell," she whispered to herself. "Less trouble for me and less noise into the bargain. At least I'm in."

That was true, but she had no idea where her quarry might have gone to ground. She was in a bedroom, thankfully unoccupied. She opened the window once more and propped it wide, knowing she might need to beat a hasty retreat. Then she tucked her knife away and rearranged her dress and veil. The specter of a black-clad, veiled woman stalking the halls of the Embassy was bound to raise a few eyebrows, but it was better than that of a knife-wielding assassin. Also, keeping her face covered would prevent easy identification later if she did manage to escape.

Coventry tiptoed to the door and tried the knob. It turned and the door opened at her touch, revealing a landing with a staircase leading down. Four more doors branched off her level, with another at the halfway point of the stairs. With nothing to tell her the correct path, she went to the first door on her left.

It, too, was unlocked. She eased it open and saw the glow of firelight. A small, merry blaze burned in the fireplace, illuminating a larger and more impressive bedroom than the one she had just left. The bed was a massive canopy structure, draped with heavy velvet curtains. The floor was richly carpeted, the furnishings intricate and expensive.

A man sat by the fire, his back to the door. She saw the crown of a bald head above the chair back. That alone told her he was not Dmitri, for the big Russian had a full, thick head of hair. This man was older and smaller. His head was bowed, either in sleep or concentration.

This was likely the Russian Ambassador, Coventry realized. What would he think if he saw her creeping about? She stepped back and began to close the door again.

"*Likho!*" a woman gasped.

Coventry froze. The voice had come from the bed. A young woman was propped against the pillows, blankets clutched to her breast, a look of terror in her eyes as she stared at the black-mantled apparition in the doorway.

Coventry had not the first idea who or what *Likho* was. Her impulse was to shut the door and run. But the old man had already stood, springing to his feet and looking first toward the bed, then the door. He was a stately-looking gentleman with a neat goatee and mustache, clad in a dressing gown. He wore a pair of wire-rimmed spectacles and fine wool slippers. In one hand he held a pipe, smoke drifting up from its bowl. In the other was a leather-bound book.

The three of them held the tableau for a few breathless moments. The young woman in the bed cowered back, hiding her face behind the blankets. She was babbling something in Russian that sounded like a prayer.

The old gentleman's face darkened. He took a step toward Coventry and made an angry gesture with his pipe, thrusting it her direction as if it were a dagger. He said something in a sharp, interrogative tone. It was in Russian, of course, and Coventry did not understand a word of it.

She decided to brazen it out. Maintaining a cold, dignified silence, she raised her arm and extended her hand theatrically, pointing toward the trembling girl. Then she began to walk toward the bed. She took care to remember her long-ago lessons in proper carriage and deportment, stepping smoothly. Her dress reached to the carpet, so she appeared to glide rather than stride, the silk of the mourning dress making a faint, sinister hissing sound.

The girl in the bed burst forth in a frantic series of entreaties. Suddenly, she gave a cry and pitched back in a dead faint.

The old gentleman had been advancing to bar Coventry's path when his companion was thus stricken. Now, faced with a dilemma, he did the honorable thing. He ran to the bedside and put his arms around the unconscious young woman, cradling her head.

Coventry seized her opportunity. She backed away, keeping the same smooth, gliding gait. Still facing the bed, she retreated through the doorway once more and drew it shut, turning the knob so the latch silently closed behind her. Then she turned from the bedroom and went to the next door. She did not know what had just happened, but dared hope she might be taken for a literal ghost. The old gentleman's first concern would be to revive his bedmate—a girl, Coventry thought, much too young for him—and only once she was recovered would he think to raise an outcry. And it was just possible he might not do that, particularly if the girl was an illicit companion. Hopefully that would be the end of the matter, at least until something else occurred. But she knew she could count on very little time.

This door was locked. Coventry drew out her trusty hairpins, but found the key was still in the lock. That meant the room was occupied, but she needed to know who was within. She swiftly took off her veil and slid the crape under the door, directly beneath the keyhole. Then she carefully poked the point of her knife into the lock, pushing the key out the far side of the door. There was a faint thump as the key fell to the floor, landing on the veil. Then she drew the veil back under the door. The key came with it. A moment more and she had opened the door.

She was greeted with the sound of snoring, a most comforting noise. Closing the door behind her, she went to the bed and looked down. The room had no light, so it was hard to see the face of the sleeping man, but she could tell this fellow was too fat-faced and soft to be Dmitri. He was some secretary or Embassy functionary, she guessed, and of no concern to her. She pocketed the key, knowing that many doors in a house could often be opened by the same key, and took her leave, replacing her veil.

The alarm had not yet been sounded, so she believed she had correctly gauged the old man's intentions. She went to the final door on the upper landing and found it opened onto a hallway lined with closets on the right. Halfway down its length was a half-flight of four steps, atop which were doors on either side.

Her heart was pounding, but Coventry was not truly frightened. It was always better to act than to react. She was here by choice. Ergo, what had she to fear? The logic was slippery, but so long as it gave her hope, what did that matter? She made her way down the hall, ignoring the closets.

As she climbed the short flight of steps, she heard the mutter of male voices through the door to her right. They were speaking their outlandish babble, but she could tell there were two men and they sounded angry. Light shone through the keyhole and under the door. The men were definitely up and about. She made her way to the door and pressed her ear against it.

She learned nothing of use. It was all so much gibberish to her. But the longer she listened, the more certain she was that one of the men was Dmitri. So the first stage of her night's work was done. She had located him. That had been the easy part. Now she needed to attract his attention and get him to pursue her. That, come to think of it, should not prove terribly difficult either.

Coventry gently tried the doorknob. It was locked, but her purloined key fit perfectly. She swung the door open to reveal one more bedroom. This one was less well-furnished than those she had previously entered. The beds had low, single-occupant mattresses. A plain wooden table with two chairs stood before the hearth. There sat Dmitri and Yuri, much the worse for wear, examining a map of London. A bottle of vodka, a pair of drinking glasses, and Dmitri's knife lay beside the map.

"Don't be downcast, lads," she said cheerily, flipping up her veil to reveal her features. "I'm not so bloody hard to find."

Coventry savored a brief, delicious moment of stunned disbelief on the part of the two men. Yuri's face was a mask of clotted blood, a bandage wrapped around his left eye. Whisper had done his desperate work well. Dmitri was intact save for his right foot, which was swathed in bloodstained cloth.

"*Suka.*"

Dmitri said it in a soft, almost reverent voice, but Coventry did not think it was a complimentary word. She puckered her lips and blew him a kiss. Then she took to her heels.

She had guessed, correctly, that Dmitri's wounded foot would slow him. But she had reckoned without Yuri. He might only have one good eye, but his feet were in perfect order and he was quicker than he looked. With an oath he made to grab her, and she only just made it out into the hallway ahead of him. His momentum carried him into the far wall. He rebounded from it, snarling and vicious.

Coventry ran. She sprinted back the way she had come, her blithe confidence evaporating. Her clever plan, now that she was caught in the midst of it, seemed suddenly quite foolish. She made it down the short flight of stairs, taking all four steps in a single flying stride. She came down wrong in the dim lighting, landing hard. There was a sudden, wrenching pain in her ankle that brought tears to her eyes. But she dared not, she could not stop. She ran through the pain, the two men thundering on behind her. All around, she heard muffled cries of surprise as the house came awake.

She reached the landing, not sparing a moment to glance behind. In front of her, the door to the master bedroom flew open. There stood the bald old gentleman. He need only take two paces to his right in order to block her path, but he stood as though rooted to the floor, amazed. She rushed past him in a stumbling run, through the door to the room by which she had entered the Embassy.

A hand caught at her shoulder. The fingers slipped and slid over the silk of the dress, finding no purchase. Coventry raced for the window. She remembered the jutting spikes of the fence below. Dare she jump? Could she clear them?

As she braced for the leap, something caught the toe of her shoe. She tripped and tumbled, banging her head against the bedroom wall. Yuri had flung himself in a headlong lunge, just catching her foot, the same way Finn had done in the Horrocks house. Now he came up on his hands and knees and scrambled toward her.

She drew back her foot and planted the heel of her shoe square in his good eye, stomping his face as hard as she could. Yuri howled and fell on his side, writhing on the carpet, hands over his face, momentarily blinded. But Dmitri was coming on fast, in spite of his injury. Coventry heard him on the landing.

He appeared in the doorway, brandishing his knife. Coventry rolled onto her knees, got her feet under her, grabbed the hem of her skirts in one hand, and sprang for the window. She pushed off the sill with her good foot and jumped.

There was a moment of breathless exhilaration. The cold night mist caressed her burning face. She felt she was flying, that she could simply sail on into the night, up past the moon and stars. Then gravity asserted its iron grip and she plunged down in a descending arc. She saw fog, the spikes of the fence flashed by close enough to brush her toes, and then the hard cobblestones of the London street rushed up to meet her.

She tucked her shoulder and tried to roll with the impact, but her bad ankle buckled as she landed. She screamed at the sudden, awful pain of it. She bumped, tumbled, and sprawled, every part of her jarring against the stones. She ended on her back, staring up at nothing but fog. There she lay, unable for the moment to rise, her every joint and muscle crying out, eyes streaming with tears of pain and exhaustion.

It might have been a minute or an hour later when she heard the clatter of footfalls on the cobbles. Four men appeared in her field of vision. Tears had blurred her sight and it took her a moment to recognize Dmitri and Yuri, together with a pair of stony-faced Russian soldiers.

Yuri's unbandaged eye had swollen nearly shut, but he gave her a stare of such malevolence from the slitted pupil that she quailed. Dmitri, however, was smiling, and that was worse.

"Stupid *suka*," he said. "What, you think you come into our house now? Very well, I invite you in. We have nice, long talk."

Where was Finn? Hadn't he heard her come out? Hadn't he heard her cry? Had he abandoned her? Coventry felt fresh tears, tears of rage. She was mostly angry at herself. How could she have trusted a man, after all she had been through? She had known better. This was her own fault.

Dmitri gestured to the two soldiers and gave them a curt order in Russian. They stooped to take hold of her arms.

"That's far enough, lads."

Finn Farrell stepped out of the mist. His truncheon was in his hand. A line of London coppers materialized behind him, barring the way back to the Russian Embassy, forming a half-circle around Coventry and her opponents. Two of the Bobbies bore lanterns that pierced the fog with their light. Finn's pair of detectives held their revolvers ready.

"Officer," Dmitri said, sketching a polite half-bow. "This woman, she is thief and house-breaker. She breaks into our Embassy tonight. I think she is spy."

"Serious charges," Finn said. "And we'll be needing to investigate them. Why don't you come down to the Yard with us and we'll sort this whole business out?"

"This is Russian business," Dmitri said, pointing to the Embassy. "We take care of it here."

"This is London," Finn said firmly, pointing his truncheon at the cobblestones.

"I will not come to your police station," Dmitri said.

"If you'll not come willingly, I'm arresting you," Finn said.

"For what?" The Russian was incredulous.

"Murder."

Dmitri laughed. "You cannot do this! I work with Embassy. I am diplomat! You cannot arrest me!"

"That's not entirely correct," Finn said. "Detective Thomas, you're well-versed in the law, aye?"

"That's right, Detective Farrell," said one of the other detectives.

"What's the law got to say about this particular question?"

"You'd be referring to the Diplomatic Privileges Act of 1708," Thomas said. "It says that civil proceedings against diplomats, public ministers, and their domestic servants are null and void."

"I am servant of Russian Ambassador," Dmitri said triumphantly.

"Ah, grand," Finn said. "So you've papers attesting to that about you?"

"Of course not! Papers are in Embassy!"

"Ah," Finn said. "See, that's a wee problem. If a lad, without papers, feels free to assault a young lady in London, what are we to do about that? I've an idea. We'll just take you and your lad here down to the Yard. Your Ambassador can come and collect you there. If he vouches for you, we've no problem. Those two uniformed lads can go. They're clearly soldiers of the Czar, they've done nothing I know of, and they're no concern of ours."

Dmitri's brows drew down thunderously. "Be careful, policeman," he said. "I am going nowhere with you."

Finn sighed. "All right, lads," he said to the other coppers. "Get the bracelets on these two. I'll take the responsibility."

"You are making terrible mistake," Dmitri said. But he did not resist as the police surrounded and disarmed him.

"We'll see," Finn said. "You all right, lass?"

Coventry nodded shakily. Seeing his expression of concern, and his extended hand, she put out her own hand and let him help her to her feet.

At that moment, another light emerged. It was borne by a Russian soldier. Three more soldiers ringed the old, bearded man Coventry had seen earlier, still in his dressing gown and slippers. Dmitri, in the process of being handcuffed by one of the Bobbies, looked up with obvious relief. He sent a rapid volley of Russian the way of the older man.

The gray-haired man looked steadily at Dmitri, no expression on his face. Then he glanced at Coventry, and finally his gaze came to rest on Finn.

"Your name, sir?" the old Russian asked.

"Detective Farrell, sir," Finn said, bowing politely. "Your servant."

"Ambassador Sidorov, sir," the Russian said.

"This lad says he's one of yours," Finn said.

"For what is he arrested, may I ask?" Sidorov inquired.

"Murder, sir. He killed the Honorable Bartleby Horrocks, Minister of Parliament. This other lad helped him."

Sidorov nodded slowly. "I see. A most serious accusation."

Coventry, leaning on Finn's arm, looked from face to face, trying to discover what was happening. There was some game being played here, but she did not know the rules. Dmitri looked smug. Finn looked coldly angry. Sidorov was unreadable.

"I know nothing of this matter," Sidorov said abruptly. "And I do not know either of these men. I do not know their names, nor their purposes in London. I only know that my household has been disturbed tonight, my people badly frightened. I trust this disturbance will not be repeated?"

"Absolutely not, sir," Finn said.

The smugness drained from Dmitri's face, leaving only bewilderment and growing fear. *"Posol Sidorov, ser!"* he cried.

"Good evening, sir," Sidorov said, giving Finn a stiff bow and ignoring Dmitri altogether. He turned back toward the Embassy. His uniformed soldiers went with him.

"There goes your diplomatic immunity, lad," Finn said to Dmitri. Yuri, at his companion's side, just whimpered and hung his head. "Now, you're coming with me."

Chapter 15

"How's the leg?" Finn asked. "Would you like me to take a look?"

"It's not polite to ask to see a girl's ankle," Coventry said.

The hour was going on midnight. They were in Finn's office at Scotland Yard. Coventry remembered only a little of the omnibus ride back to the police station. She had been very weary. As the shock and fear of the evening's events had worn off, what was left of her energy had drained out of her. She vaguely recalled Finn carrying her up the stairs, like a bridegroom carrying his betrothed over the threshold. Then she must have fallen asleep. When she awoke, she was curled in an old leather chair in the corner, a woolen blanket over her shoulders, Finn at his desk watching her. The room was empty save for the two of them.

He laughed quietly. "Aye, that was rude of me. I apologize. But you've had rather a rough night. Is there anything you're needing?"

"A cup of tea wouldn't come amiss," she said. "Or a glass of spirits."

He picked up a teacup from his desk. "It's not the best," he warned her, coming around the desk and handing her the cup. "But it's hot. I thought you might be wanting a cup."

"Bloody mind reader, that's what you are," she muttered, wrapping her hands around the cup and sipping. Delightful warmth flooded into her. She shivered deliciously.

"Better?" he asked.

Coventry nodded. "Why are you being so bloody nice to me?"

"Why shouldn't I be?"

"You're a copper."

He raised an eyebrow. "So?"

"Coppers are bastards, the whole lot of you."

"Come now, that's a bit much. We saved you from the Russians, didn't we?"

"Took your damned time about it. You let me think they had me!"

"I had to work my way around behind them, make certain they'd no chance to scurry back into the Embassy. I'm sorry if I frightened you. But in fairness, we'd no idea where you'd be coming out and when, and it took a wee bit of time to find you in the fog. Still, all's well as ends well, aye?"

"I suppose," she grumbled. "If it truly is over. What happens now?"

"Now Dmitri and Yuri stew in their cells and await their fate."

"How did you know the Ambassador would turn his back on them?"

He grinned. "I'm no politician, Miss Adams, but I know how they think. I gave the blighter a choice. Either he denied the lads were his agents, or he claimed them. If he claimed them, he'd be admitting his government assassinated a Minister of Parliament. That's an act of war. It would also lead to Mr.

Sidorov owing a very awkward explanation to his Czar. He'd be risking his position, and likely his own head. Under the circumstances, he made the obvious choice and tossed his bully-boys to the wolves."

"Hard luck on them," she commented without much sympathy.

"Oh aye, but that's the fate of such as they," Finn said. "That's what happens when you give your loyalty to the government. It's a road that only leads one direction."

"You've sworn an oath to your government," she reminded him.

"I've sworn an oath to the law," he corrected her. "I'd not commit murder for my Queen."

"Can you prove they killed Horrocks?"

"They've already confessed."

"What?" Coventry sat bolt upright. The blanket slipped from her shoulders. "Dmitri's as hard a man as they come. What in blazes did you do to him?"

Finn looked distinctly smug. "Oh, it wasn't difficult. If he'd been alone, I doubt he'd have broken. But with two of them, that's a simple trick."

She looked at him expectantly. "Go on, then," she said. "Explain. Every bloke loves to show off his cleverness."

He shrugged. "I put the lads in separate rooms where they couldn't hear one another. Then I told each of them that the first one to confess would get Transportation. The one who didn't talk would have his neck stretched at Tyburn. Then I gave them a few minutes to think it over, so each could imagine the other lad spilling his secrets. By the time I got back in each room, the both of them were practically falling over themselves to confess."

"No honor among murderers," she murmured.

"When you take away everything else, what's left is the will to survive," he said.

"I know," she said with feeling. "So which one did the actual stabbing?"

"Yuri."

"Really? Dmitri seemed more the sort to me."

"Oh, Yuri's a coward, right enough," Finn agreed. "In your experience, Miss Adams, have you more to fear from a brave man or a coward?"

"A coward," she said, thinking of Handsome Hal. "A brave man won't stab you in the back. He'll at least do it to your face."

"Precisely. Dmitri was the lookout, Yuri did the killing. They rented the room next door. They'd been watching Mr. Horrocks quite some time, learning his habits. They knew he liked to pick up young... ah... women..."

Finn paused. His cheeks flushed.

"Finn, I know exactly why he asked me into his carriage," Coventry said. "That was part of the game. You needn't fear wounding my delicate feelings."

He cleared his throat. "Simply putting a knife in the lad might have led to questions," he said. "They needed a patsy, a sap to take the fall for them. So while Mr. Horrocks was out looking for a lovely lass, Yuri and Dmitri were getting ready to make it look like the lass had done for him. Dmitri kept an eye on the hallway and Yuri waited under the bed."

Coventry swallowed. "Under the bed?" she repeated faintly. "He was there? The whole time?"

"Oh, aye," Finn said. "Just waiting his opportunity. It's as well you left. If you'd stayed the night, he'd have waited till you were asleep, stabbed the both of you, and made it look like a lover's quarrel. He was a mite surprised when you drugged the lad and left, but Dmitri figured it would only be easier to make you look guilty, seeing as you'd robbed him. The whole thing was quite convenient, from their point of view."

"I see," she said. "So which one hangs and which goes to Australia?"

"Both bastards hang," he said grimly. "And I'll be there to make sure it happens."

"But you said the first one to talk would live," she said.

"I lied."

She stared at him. "Finn..." she began.

"They're murderers," he said. "There's but one penalty for stabbing a Minister of Parliament. They're lucky we don't draw and quarter the swine as we used to."

"But... they were following orders," she said. "Unless the Ambassador really didn't know what they were up to."

"Oh, he knew," Finn said. "In fact, I'd say the whole thing was his idea."

"Then why isn't he cooling his heels in Newgate?"

"I can't arrest the Russian Ambassador. That would lead to war with Russia for certain. Why's this troubling you? Those gobshites tried to kill you."

"I know," she said. "It's just not bloody fair. They might have been the hands, but Sidorov was the brain, and he gets away with it?"

"You're getting away with more than a few things, come to that," he said gently. "Are you really wanting justice to triumph in all things?"

"But... But that means Sidorov wins!" she exclaimed. "Damn it all, he got his bloody treaty! He's going to get medals and... and dinners in his honor and... he's got a girl less than half his age in his bed!"

"What?" Finn asked. "What girl?"

That reminded Coventry. "What's a *Likho*?" she asked.

"I've no idea. Is that a Russian word?"

"Perhaps. The girl in Sidorov's room called me that when I showed up in my black dress and veil. I think she thought I was some sort of ghost."

Finn laughed again. "I daresay!" he said. "That must have been a sight to see! In your weeds, you looked a right bane-sidhe."

"A which?"

"Bane-sidhe. Banshee, if you'd rather. I've told you of them before. We've plenty of them in Ireland, so they say, though I've never seen one. I must say, you look rather less ghostly now. That tea's put some color back in your cheeks. It's done you a spot of good, I'll warrant."

"Speaking of warrants..." she said.

"Oh aye," he said. "It's taken care of. Now that we've a pair of confessed murderers, there's little interest in dragging you to the Old Bailey. In fact, given the evidence of other criminals being in that room, it's unlikely anyone can prove you stole anything. The worst they could do is throw you in Bridewell for prostitution."

Coventry laughed bitterly. "And you'd call that justice? I'm no tart, not anymore."

"I know who you are."

"Do you, now?"

"Aye."

Finn was looking straight into her eyes with a very odd expression on his face. Coventry felt another shiver run through her, almost of fear. She did not know what the Irishman was thinking, but the way he was looking at her made her distinctly uncomfortable.

"Finn?" she asked softly, needing to distract him.

"Aye?" He did not blink.

"Thank you."

"What is it you're thanking me for, Miss Adams?"

"You believed me. You helped me. Not many blokes have done as much for me these past years."

He blinked finally, breaking the spell. "Glad to be of service, Miss Adams. And I do apologize again for the knock on the head."

"I'd say it makes us about even." She smiled and put out a hand, gently brushing his face. The black eye she'd given him had turned very dark.

He nodded. "Fair play to you, darling. But I think I may be a mite ahead. I did save your life. Twice, by my reckoning."

Coventry licked her lips. "Well, that's true enough," she said. "And I don't like to be in a man's debt. So I suppose I'd best pay you back."

"I've no need of your stolen money," he said. "I live cheaply enough. Besides, you can't go offering coin to a copper. That's a crime."

"I wasn't talking about money," she said. She stood and went to the office door, bolting it. Then, before Finn realized what she was doing, she hiked up her skirts and settled herself across his lap.

"Good God," Finn blurted. Then she bent her head and kissed him, cutting off whatever else he was trying to say.

It was far from the worst kiss Coventry Adams had ever experienced. Finn was surprised, so he did not participate much, but his face was relatively clean and he was neither brutal nor coarse. His mustache tickled her face, but she did not mind. She leaned into him, letting him feel all of her, offering herself to him. She felt him responding, returning the kiss, moving to meet her.

She welcomed the moment. The act of coupling held no fear for her. He would not hurt her, she knew that now. It would draw him closer to her. Perhaps it would even be pleasant.

Then something changed. He shifted, pushing her away. Coventry did not understand. She pressed closer, more urgently. But he became more definite, more determined in his turn, breaking off the kiss. He pushed her away, gently but firmly, and held her by the shoulders, at arm's length.

"What's the matter?" she demanded, confused and angry. "I'm not good enough for you, is that it? Just a bit of East End street trash? Are you too bloody proud to take a roll in the gutter?"

"Nay, that's not it," he said. He seemed embarrassed now.

"It's not that you don't think I'm pretty," she said, flicking her eyes down to his trousers. "I could tell."

Finn turned bright red. "Nay, that's not it either. This whole business, it's not right. This isn't how it ought to go."

"How ought it to go then, Finn Farrell?" she demanded, twisting off his lap and standing up. "Why don't you tell me, with your great experience of women? Because from what I've seen, this is exactly how it goes! You did me a good turn. I was trying to thank you, to pay a debt! The least you could do is accept it like a gentleman!"

"A gentleman? This isn't what a gentleman does."

"This is what every gentleman does! Get him alone, turn down the light, strip off his britches, and every gentleman's the same! They only want one thing from a girl like me! They want it so much, they pay to get it! Except you. I offer you a free ride and you throw it back in my face? What makes you so bloody high and mighty?"

"I've no experience whatever of... of women of the sort you used to be," he said softly.

"Oh, well that's just marvelous. I won't sully your spotless reputation any further." Coventry turned on her heel and reached for the bolt to unlock the door.

"Felicia, please."

The words stopped her in her tracks. She was frozen, hand still outstretched, fingertips just touching the cold iron of the bolt. She did not turn, but remained staring at the door.

"What did you call me?" she asked in a low, trembling voice.

"Felicia Fox-Brooke," he said, as if reading from a book. "Daughter of Lord Hamilton Fox-Brooke. Disappeared from Farringdon Street Station in London, February 19th, 1868. Believed abducted. Miss Fox-Brooke was sixteen years of age at the time of her disappearance. She is roughly five feet tall, weighing approximately one hundred pounds. She is slight of frame and very slender, with pale skin, blue eyes, and red-brown hair of unusual color and luster. The Metropolitan Police investigated the disappearance, but have to date been unable either to account for her movements or to locate her remains. Lord Fox-Brooke has offered a reward of three thousand pounds for her safe return, or for definite knowledge of her fate."

"Stop," Coventry whispered. Her hand, suspended in air, was shaking. "Please, stop."

Finn came to stand behind her, slightly to one side. "Felicia?" he said in a tone of heartbreaking gentleness.

"Stop calling me that," she said.

He touched her shoulder. She flinched.

He hastily withdrew his hand. "I meant no offense," he said. "If I've hurt you, I'm sorry."

"How did you know?" she asked.

"I wasn't certain until just now, seeing your reaction. But a few things have been troubling me about you."

She turned, finally, to face him, setting her back against the door. "What business was it of yours, anyway?" she snapped, mustering all the defiance left to her.

"You're clearly an educated lass," he said, ignoring the question. "You've some knowledge of the Classics. You've no Russian or Turkish, but I'll wager you've a fair sense of Latin and French. Greek, maybe, as well."

Coventry glared at him and said nothing.

"In hospital, when you awoke, you'd lost your Cockney," he went on. "You cover it well, but your speech is high-born.

I knew your da must be a toff, probably a lord of some sort. A lass like that doesn't just fall out of the sky and land in the East End. Poor lasses come and go, but rich ones leave a trail. You'd a history, and I suspected I'd find it in the files here at the Yard."

Finn paused, searching her face for confirmation or acknowledgment. She offered none.

"My theory was you'd run off from home," he continued after a moment. "Perhaps you'd been trying to escape an arranged match. I was wrong about that. But there aren't so many missing daughters of lords, even in a place as big as London, and you've a memorable face. Once I started looking, it didn't take long. That was just as well, as I'd more than a few important matters to attend to. A political assassination, to begin with."

"Why bother, then?" she burst out. "This was none of your affair. You had no right to meddle!"

"I'd a duty," he said sharply. "A duty to a father who lost his daughter, a man without even the cold comfort of a gravestone to remember her by! You're not the only one touched by this, Miss Fox-Brooke."

"You think I don't know that?" she retorted. "So I suppose you're off to collect your reward. At least you're getting a better price than Judas did! Three thousand pounds is a sight better than thirty pieces of silver!"

"I told you, I've no desire for ill-gotten money," he snapped. "Not yours, and certainly not your da's. You think I'd take coin in exchange for you? You think I'm a bloody slave-trader, or one of those so-called gentlemen who dishonored you? At least I'm thinking of your da's feelings, which is more than you seem capable of."

"Did you ever think, maybe I wasn't only thinking of myself? That maybe I was trying to protect Mother and Father?" Tears of rage and tears of grief mingled bitterly in Coventry's eyes and overflowed onto her cheeks.

That stopped Finn short. "What do you mean? Did someone threaten your family?"

"Nothing like that," she said. "Though I wouldn't put it past a bastard like Hal. Try to think like a woman, just for a minute, Finn! Or if you can't do that, at least try to think like a man with something to lose. You want to know what happened to me? I was taken, gulled by a slick-talking cove on the lookout for fresh meat. He beat me until I did what he told me. My back has scars from his lash. You want to see them?"

Finn looked sickened. "Nay," he whispered. "I've seen the like on other girls, ones we've found floating in the Thames."

"He sold me to an old gentleman," she went on relentlessly, giving the last word a scornful twist in her mouth. "You know what they say? That having a maiden cures a man of the French pox? It's not bloody true, but they try it anyway. Twenty pounds, that's what my virtue was worth. After that, of course, I was just another whore. He kept me tied to a bed most of the time. You want to know what I went for then? Sixpence a tumble. A shilling if the gentleman wanted something special, the sort of things his wife wouldn't do for him. I'd earn Hal two crowns, most nights. Not that I ever saw a hay-penny of that myself."

"Two bloody crowns," Finn muttered. "For lying down for those bastards." His hand went into his coat and wrapped around the handle of his truncheon. His knuckles whitened on the hardwood shaft.

"Every night, except when I was ill," Coventry confirmed. "I've had the mercury treatments twice. Not to mention the other nastiness a tart has to endure. All for a few moments' sweaty grappling with *gentlemen*."

"Enough," Finn said. "I know what happens."

"I'm sorry if hearing about my life's hard on your delicate ears. You brought this up, damn you. Are you sparing my sensibilities or your own?"

"My apologies," he said. "I've no right—"

"You know what I'd be, if I suddenly turned up at home?" she interrupted. "A laughingstock or a charity case! And I'll not be either. I was supposed to make a good match, marry some fine earl's son. Who'd have me now? No wedding bells for me, Finn. One of my friends recognized me the other day, don't you know? And I was terrified. I managed to play the whole thing off as a mistake, cut her dead, crushed her with bloody etiquette. And why do you think I did that? You think she'd still be my friend once she knew the truth?"

Coventry's face contorted angrily. "She'd pity me, of course. They'd all pity me." Her voice took on a false, mocking sweetness. "'Poor, dear Felicia! Did you hear what happened to her, poor thing? Now she's ruined, of course, and just think what it's done to her poor mother and father. How can they ever bear the shame?' They'd all pretend to be shocked and sad, but they'd whisper about me behind their hands at all the parties. Not that I'd ever be invited to any of those. Society has doors, Finn, and those doors would be slammed in my face. Shame is catching, as bad as consumption. You catch it, the next thing you know, it's all over your friends and family. You want me to think of my father? I am thinking of him! He'd be ruined along with me! And knowing his worst fears had come true? Better he think me dead. The truth might kill him!"

Finn's eyes were soft, and to Coventry's surprise she saw that he, too, was fighting back tears. He reached toward her.

"I am so sorry, Felicia," he said.

She slapped his hand away. "I don't want your damned pity! Haven't you heard a word I said? I'm not Felicia! I can't be! Felicia died in Whitechapel three years ago! I can't dwell in the past. I can't live on memories and bloody compassion! I've got to move forward, make my own way."

"There's other paths you might take," he said. "You needn't lie and steal."

"What other paths?" she flung back contemptuously.

"You've done a great service to the Crown," he said. "And to Scotland Yard. I'd never have caught Mr. Horrocks's murderers without you."

"So you think I should be a copper? Got many female Bobbies at the Yard, do you?"

He shook his head. "Nay, that's not possible, I fear. Maybe someday, but not in this day and age."

"What, then? You're not offering to take care of me yourself, make me your mistress. You'll not have me that way, you've made that clear enough."

Finn blinked and blushed again. "Felicia—Coventry, I assure you, you've no lack of charms, and I'm no more immune to them than the next lad."

"Could've fooled me." But her voice lost just a little of its angry edge.

"Flesh needn't be a transaction," he said. "I know it's been that way with every man who's... been with you. But I swear to

God, we're not all like that. I'll not take you in payment, nor out of obligation, not even if you're offering."

"You're a bloody monk, then," she guessed. "Have you never taken a tumble with a lass?"

"That's beside the point, and a very impolite question."

"Haven't you noticed, Finn? I'm not exactly polite."

He smiled faintly. "Aye, that's crossed my notice. All you need know is, I'm no Shylock. I'll not take payment in flesh, by the pound or otherwise."

"Then what do you want me to do?"

"The Yard was offering two hundred fifty pounds for you, not two hours ago," he said.

"I'd noticed. And my father offered three thousand. But I can't very well sell myself and collect. What of it?"

"Your face isn't the only one on that wall. And coppers can't collect rewards for bringing in criminals."

Then she understood. "You want me to help you nick some babblings and earn some bangers when you catch them."

"Beg pardon?"

She sighed. "Babbling brooks, crooks. Bangers and mash, cash," she translated. "Bloody hell, Finn, haven't you spent any time in the East End at all?"

"The point of the jargon is to keep lads like me from understanding it," he said, smiling more broadly. "What do you say, Coventry Adams?"

"You'll keep my secret?" she asked, almost succeeding in keeping the pleading note out of her voice.

It was his turn to sigh. "Aye. Though I think you're making a grave error, I'll not betray you."

"And you won't ship me off to Australia?"

"You'll stop robbing gentlemen," he countered. "Or you'll find yourself on a ship one of these days."

Coventry's jaw worked. "A girl's got to eat," she muttered sulkily.

"If we work together to get you an income, you'll not be needing to pick pockets," he said.

"Fair enough," she said. "And what cut will you be wanting? Half, I suppose?"

"I told you, we can't collect rewards. I'll be doing my duty, you'll be getting your living, and we'll be stopping bad lads from harming more folk."

"I do this for you and we're even, yes?"

"If you insist on thinking of it like that, aye."

"Are we needing a contract?"

"A handshake's good enough for this Irishman."

She extended a hand. "Then you've got a deal, Finn Farrell." She paused. "Until I start making money the way you're wanting, I don't suppose you could lend me a few quid? I really am flat broke."

Chapter 16

Coventry climbed the alley stairs carrying her old portmanteau. Finn had declined to lend her any money—the lad was a sharp one, after all, and knew better than to expect repayment—but he had said that, since she was no longer wanted by the police, it would be immoral to confiscate her belongings. Accordingly, he had returned her traveling case to her.

She opened the door. "Morning, Slinky," she called.

"Oh, no," Slinky McGee said. "Not you again! I've not half cleaned the bloodstains off the floor! Nick's still resting at home, more dead than alive, thanks to those foreigners what followed you here. I've got coves scared to come in for a hand of cards. They'd rather be home with their wives, if you can believe it! You're nothing but trouble, Cov. On your way, and take your bad luck with you!"

Coventry gave him her most winsome, charming smile. "Slinky, don't be like that," she said. "Haven't I always paid my dues, on time and in full? Can you say the same of all your tenants?"

"It's not about the coin," he grumbled. "Big bloody Russians coming in here, knocking my boys on the head. 'Taint right! The government ought to do something."

"The government did," she said. "You won't see those particular Russians again. They've made a date with Jack Ketch and they'll swing for certain."

Slinky looked marginally more cheerful. "That's a bit of all right, I reckon. But I can't be having such goings-on in my place. Besides, I've already let out your room."

"I was paid through the end of the week," she said. "Left the coin on the mattress along with the key."

"And I told you, it's not about the coin."

"Any man says that, he just means there isn't enough coin yet," she said, stirring the contents of her handbag. An enticing jingling sound emanated. She'd promised herself it had been her last pickpocketing jaunt, but habits were hard to break, and the well-to-do lad she'd nicked the coin from would hardly starve for lack of it.

Slinky's interest sharpened. "And you promise that other business is done with?"

"Over and done," she assured him, placing a shilling on the bar.

His eyes followed the coin. "Well, in point of fact, I haven't quite let your room yet. But there's interest."

Another coin joined the first. "Do tell," she said sweetly.

"Here's your key," Slinky said, handing it over with one hand while he swept the coins toward him with the other. "It's good having you back, Cov. You're a good girl."

"No," she said, still smiling. "I'm not, and you know it. Say, how did you know they were Russians?"

"From their jargon," he said. "Back in the old days, when I served before the mast, my ship worked the North Sea. We ran into a fair number of Muscovites and I learned a bit of their patter."

"Did you ever hear of a *Likho*?" she asked.

"Where'd you hear that?" Slinky asked sharply.

"From a girl who thought she'd seen a ghost," Coventry said. "Why? What's it mean?"

"That's a bad word to use in front of a gambler, Cov," he said somberly. "A *Likho* is a sort of bad-luck spirit. Sailors talked about her. It looks like a woman, dressed in black. Usually she's got just one eye. She latches onto you and rides around on your back, or she gets passed around like a bad coin, cheating everyone she meets. You didn't see her, did you?"

"No," Coventry said, thinking it unwise to tell Slinky she'd been mistaken for one of the spirits. Sailors could be a very superstitious lot. She wondered about Sidorov's girl and what the young woman might have thought she'd done to earn the attentions of an evil spirit. That, at least, explained why the poor thing had fainted.

Coventry went down the hall and unlocked the door to her old room. It was odd how returning to even the humblest of bedrooms, this chilly little garret, could feel like reaching a safe haven. That safety was an illusion, as she knew perfectly well, but she embraced it nonetheless, stepping into the room and inhaling the musty, dusty, familiar scent of the place.

She stopped short. The room was already occupied. Someone was settled on the bed.

"Whisper?" she gasped. She dropped her portmanteau and clapped a hand to her mouth.

The black cat reached out with his front paws, elevated his hindquarters, and stretched. His claws emerged from his forepaws as he yawned. Then he gave Coventry a cool, non-committal look and began washing his whiskers.

"Oh, Whisper," she said, dropping to her knees beside the bed. "I am so very sorry. It's not like I wanted to throw you in that meater's face. Only, they were going to kill me. I did what I had to. Can't you forgive me?"

Whisper continued his toilette, studiously ignoring her.

"I promise I'll never, ever do it again," she said. "If it's any consolation, you saved my life."

The cat did not appear consoled. Nor, however, did he appear particularly troubled. From his perspective, Coventry was currently beneath notice.

She sighed and rummaged through her things, finding a bit of sausage. "Here," she said, laying it on the mattress beside him.

Whisper pretended not to see the peace offering for a few moments. Then, very casually, he bent and sniffed at it. He batted the bit of meat with a paw. Then, almost too quickly for Coventry's eye to follow, he snatched it up in his mouth and leapt into the corner, out of sight.

She left him to his meal and laid her portmanteau on the bed. She unlatched it and opened it, expecting very little. In her experience, coppers were as corrupt as most men. She thought to find her clothing ripped and torn, her money stolen, her belongings thoroughly rifled.

The case was complete with everything that had been inside it. Even the banknotes and coin were untouched, though Finn had doubtless known, or suspected, their provenance.

"Too honest for his own good, that one," she muttered. "The bloke will lie to criminals, but he won't line his own pockets. And here I thought I understood men."

But she smiled as she laid out her red satin dress, smoothing the wrinkles as best she could. It certainly was pretty, though it promised more than she was prepared to deliver. She wondered what Finn would say if she was wearing it the next time they met. He'd have a hard time looking at her face, given what else would be on display.

That was nonsense, of course. Finn Farrell might think her alluring, but their relationship was to be strictly a business undertaking. He'd made that abundantly clear. It suited Coventry perfectly. She had neither the time nor the inclination to deal with other entanglements. It was just possible he was telling the truth, that he wasn't out to take advantage of her, but that made him a rare bird indeed. She intended not to trust any man farther than she must.

She hung the dress on the rod that served as a makeshift closet. Then she lay down on her back, carefully on account of her corset, and folded her hands behind her head. She thought of Bartleby Horrocks. That one's death had been no great loss, but what did it mean for the world? Would he have been able to prevent the Treaty being enacted? And if so, would it have meant another war with Russia? Had his death truly saved lives? Or had it merely postponed the reckoning? Payment might yet come due, with interest.

Such things were not her concern. She was no diplomat. Millicent Fawcett and her disciples were agitating for women to gain entry to the world of politics, but Coventry was not entirely sure why they wanted such a thing. Stuffy, boring old men with greedy eyes and grasping hands were not the sort of fellows with whom she wished to spend her days. It was enough that she had won her own freedom, a new job of sorts, and even a new friend.

"Is he, though?" she wondered aloud. She realized that, while she did not fully trust Finn, she wished to trust him. And that was dangerous. It could lead her to do foolish things like that madcap leap out of the Russian Embassy. Whatever had she been thinking? What if she had spiked herself on the fence? What if Finn had been a little too slow in arriving, or if he had not come at all?

"But he did come," she murmured. And that was after she'd blacked his eye, bloodied his face, and escaped from him twice.

Something brushed her wrist. She jumped in surprise, twisting on the mattress to face a pair of glass-green eyes not six inches from her own. Whisper stared at her, unblinking, for the space of five breaths. Then he butted his head against her hand.

She stroked his head, feeling his ears flatten against his skull. She moved her hand down his neck and caressed his back. His spine arched and his tail went up like a flag, waving with pleasure. The throaty rumble of his purring began, deep in his chest.

He curled himself into a ball and lay down in the hollow between Coventry's arm and her body. She rested her hand lightly on his warm, furry form and smiled. All was forgiven.

"I've still got you," she whispered. "And you've got me."

And for that moment, in that place, it was enough.

London Slang Glossary

Anointing: A good beating, one that might require the application of salve afterward.

Babbling: Cockney rhyming slang: Babbling Brook = Crook.

Bangers: Cockney rhyming slang: Bangers and Mash = Cash.

Batty-fang: To thrash thoroughly.

Bees: Cockney rhyming slang: Bees and Honey = Money.

Berk: Cockney rhyming slang: Berkely Hunt = Cunt. (Extremely impolite.)

Box-Man: Criminal slang for a criminal who breaks into safes.

Butcher's: Cockney rhyming slang: Butcher's Hook = Look.

Copper: Cop, policeman.

Cove: A chap or fellow.

Cows: Cockney rhyming slang: Cows and Kisses = Missus (Wife).

Dash: Cockney rhyming slang: Dot and Dash = Moustache.

Donnybrook: Irish slang for a fight or disturbance.

Drum: Cockney rhyming slang: Drum and Fife = Knife.

Frying Pan: Cockney rhyming slang: Frying Pan = Old Man (Husband).

Gibface: A particularly ugly person.

Grasshoppers: Cockney rhyming slang: Grasshoppers = Coppers (Police).

Hay-penny Knee-trembler: A cheap purchase from a low-class prostitute, usually transacted standing up in the nearest alley and completed as quickly as possible.

Hornswoggler: A fraud or cheat.

Hugger-Mugger: Sneaky or underhanded.

Jack Ketch: Nickname for any London executioner.

Jollocks: A fat man.

Lady: Cockney rhyming slang. Lady from Bristol = Pistol.

Meater: A coward.

Mutton Shunter: A policeman tasked with hassling prostitutes.

Newgate: Notorious London prison.

Night Flower: A prostitute.

Old Bailey, The: The criminal court of England and Wales. Named after the street on which it stands.

Pigeon-Livered: A coward.

Ratbag: A rogue or scoundrel; a term of general abuse.

Roller: A woman who poses as a prostitute for the purpose of robbing would-be clients.

Tart: A prostitute.

Toff: A derogatory term for a rich man, or a member of the upper class.

Took the Shilling: Took the King's (or Queen's) Shilling means to enlist in the British Army. The original pay for a private was a shilling a day.

Transportation: Punishment for criminals in England, in which they were shipped on a one-way journey to Australia.

Turkish Delight: Cockney rhyming slang: Turkish Delight = Shite.

Tyburn Cross: Location of public executions in London.

Wagtail: A prostitute.

Here's a sneak peek from Book 2: Thief-Taker

Coming soon!

"This is your lucky night, guv," the girl said.

"I'm taking the egg, no fear," the man at her side said. He grinned at her, showing yellow-stained teeth with several gaps where their brethren had once been. He was an ill-favored fellow, cheeks pockmarked and scarred, and he stank.

The girl nestled closer to him at the faro table, leaning against his arm. She smiled brightly and tried not to breathe through her nose. The gambling hall was dark, dingy, and smoky. She herself was the most colorful thing in the place; she was wearing her red satin, the better to attract attention.

The dress was serving its purpose. The ugly lout could scarcely keep his eyes off her. She was everything he was not: young, pretty, and innocent—at least to the untrained eye. He was old by the standards of London's lower classes; forty at least. He was ugly, and certainly not innocent. But he was winning at cards, his stack of coins twice as high as it had been when he had approached the gaming table, and while the girl was obviously a harlot, that was a point in her favor as far as he was concerned.

"I'm Barney," he said. "Who might you be?"

"Round here they calls me Coventry," she said.

"Like the city?"

"Just like," she said with a slight giggle, as if he had made a witticism.

Barney guffawed, spraying spittle onto the green baize tabletop.

"Bets, gentlemen," the dealer said.

Barney slid his copper betting token onto the jack which sat in front of him. Coventry watched his movements carefully. She was no gambler, knowing all too well how heavily the odds favored the house. She also knew the dealer in this particular establishment to be a cheater. Barney was doing well at the moment, but the dealer was simply leading him to slaughter.

Coventry did not wish that to happen. The more coin in Barney's pockets, the happier she would be. So she slipped her little hand under his arm and gave it a light squeeze. As she did so, her other hand went inside his outer shirt and caressed him.

"I'd love to hang around and watch you play," she said. "You've a fine, confident way with your hands. But I've got to be working. I'd best run along. Ta, love."

She went up on tiptoes and brushed the stubble on his unshaven cheek with her lips, the barest hint of a kiss, letting her breath tickle his face with warm promise. Then she stepped away from him and walked to the door, making her hips sway beneath her skirt.

It was a calculated risk. She did not know whether he would follow her or not. But as in fishing, when stringing a lad along, it was wise to give him room to run. It made him feel in control of the situation. Blind confidence, like anger, made men stupid. And when coupled with lust, it was a potent mixture.

She was almost at the door when she heard him call to her and knew she had him. "Coventry!" he shouted. "Hold up, lass!"

Coventry pretended not to hear him. She stepped out into the alley and the Whitechapel night, drawing in a deep breath. The air still held unmentionable stenches, but at least it was slightly freer to move outside the confines of the gambling den. She walked quickly toward the corner, passing a slender man muffled in a heavy overcoat, hat pulled low over his eyes. She gave him the barest nod as she went by.

Heavy footfalls pursued her. She smelled Barney even before his heavy hand came down on her shoulder. Her flesh shrank from the touch, but she mastered the impulse to fight or flee. He spun her about to face him. The alley was narrow and their noses were barely five inches apart.

"Don't go running off like that," Barney said. "We were just starting to get on well. Here's me with coin in my pockets and you with your living to earn. How much?"

"How much for what, guv?" she asked with feigned innocence that fooled neither of them.

"Just a quick tumble," he said. "Hay-penny for a quick knee-trembler?"

He pressed closer to her, forcing her back against the soot-stained bricks.

Her heart was pounding, but she put a sly smile on her lips. "I don't come that cheap, guv," she said. "A shilling's my price, and I'm worth it."

"All right," he said, already fumbling at his trousers. "Shilling it is."

"Half a moment," she said. "Let's see the color of your coin, Barnabas Cowling."

He hauled a silver coin out of his pocket and dropped it on the cobbles. Almost before it clinked on the stone, he was groping eagerly for her. Then he froze. His wits, fogged though they were by lust and cheap grog, sounded a belated alarm.

"How do you know my name?" he asked.

"Barnabas Cowling," another voice said from just behind the man. It was the young fellow Coventry had passed a moment before. His accent was that of an Irish workingman, but the words were delivered with a firmness and authority that commanded attention.

Barney released Coventry and spun to face the other man, ignoring the girl. She was small and female and clearly no threat to him. His hands clenched into instinctive fists.

"What's this?" he demanded. "She work for you?"

"In a manner of speaking," the Irishman said. He threw back his coat, revealing the silver badge of the Metropolitan Police. His other hand came out from under the coat holding a stout wooden cudgel. "My name's Detective Farrell and here's my authority. Mr. Cowling, it's my duty to apprehend you for theft and assault. If you'll come quiet, you'll take no harm from me."

"And go meek to Tyburn?" Barney growled. "Or Australia? Not bloody likely. Call your bully-boys, or have a go yourself if you think you're hard enough."

"I'm the only copper here, lad," Farrell said. "And I've plenty of force to deal with the likes of you. You're a coward who strikes from behind. I doubt you've the guts to deal with a man face-to-face."

Barney's ugly mug twisted into a sneer. "You came down here alone?" he said. "You're a bloody fool. And tomorrow morn they'll find a foolish copper face-down in the gutter."

As he spoke, he reached into his own shirt. Then he paused. His sneer hung on his face like a crooked picture on a boarding-house wall. He felt a slight prick in his side, the point of something sharp.

"I said I was the only copper here, lad," Farrell said quietly. "I never said I was alone."

"And you'd be looking for this," Coventry added. She gave a nudge to the dagger she had stolen when her hand had slipped inside his shirt at the faro table. The point jabbed Barney's side, just below the ribs. "Best listen to the man and come quiet."

"You damned bobtail tart," Barney snarled. Heedless of danger, he swung, aiming a backhanded blow at her head.

Detective Farrell's cudgel caught him mid-swing with a whistling crack of wood against bone. Barney howled and clutched at his injured arm. Before he could recover, Farrell stepped in close, jabbed him in the belly with the end of his stick, then brought it down sharply on the back of his head as he doubled over. Barnabas Cowling went down hard, making no further sound or movement.

Farrell nudged the fallen man with the toe of his boot. "There's one of us face-down in the gutter," he mildly observed. "But it's not me. Are you all right, Miss Adams?"

"In the pink, Finn," Coventry said. "And I've told you not to bother standing on ceremony. It's plain Coventry on the street."

"That's no way to address a young lady," Finn Farrell said. As he spoke, he stooped and closed a pair of manacles around the unconscious man's wrists.

"I don't see any young ladies about," Coventry said, shooting him a warning glance. Finn was the only man in London who had seen through her disguise. He knew her real name and her family history, neither of which she wished to be spoken aloud.

"As you wish," Finn replied. "We've wanted to get our hands on this scunner for quite some time. And nicely done, getting his knife off him. Perhaps we ought to teach that trick at the Yard."

"Oh, I'm sure that would go over well with your chief," Coventry said with a twinkle in her eye. "Teaching coppers how to be pickpockets."

"Damnation, but this lad's heavy," Finn grunted. His attempt to heave the recumbent Barney met with little success.

"You really should've brought more lads," Coventry said.

Finn shook his head. "If I'd brought a crew of coppers down here, word would've got round and Cowling would've done a runner. Quick and quiet was the way to take him. Can you watch him a moment while I hail a cab?"

"Happy to," Coventry said, and that was the plain truth. Finn's departure left her ample opportunity to divest Barney of his faro winnings and other pocket money. Was it a sin to rob a man who was himself a thief? That was a question for priests and philosophers, and she was neither.

By the time Finn returned, Barney was coming to. But the prisoner was unable to do more than groan incoherently as Finn and Coventry bundled him into the cab. Finn climbed up to join him.

"I'm sorry we've no more room," the Irishman said. "I fear the hansom won't take three."

"That's quite all right," Coventry said, smiling. "I've got quite as close to him as I wished already. You two fine gentlemen can be on your way."

"And you can claim your reward at the Old Bailey in the morning," Finn said.

"Stroke of ten?" she suggested.

"I'll see you there," he promised. He tipped his hat politely, closed the cab door, and rolled away into the night.

Ready for more?

Join the Clickworks Press email list
for the latest on new releases, upcoming books and
series, behind-the-scenes details, events, and more.

Be the first to know about
new releases from Steven Henry
by signing up at
clickworkspress.com/join/steven

Don't miss out!

Visit the website below and you can sign up to receive emails whenever Steven Henry publishes a new book. There's no charge and no obligation.

https://books2read.com/r/B-A-QTGF-MEPCH

BOOKS 2 READ

Connecting independent readers to independent writers.

About the Author

Steven Henry learned how to read almost before he learned how to walk. Ever since he began reading stories, he wanted to put his own on the page. He lives a very quiet and ordinary life in Minnesota with his wife and dog.

Read more at https://clickworkspress.com/join/erin/.